Tales
Worth
Retelling

GLOBE BOOK COMPANY, INC.

NEW YORK / CHICAGO / CLEVELAND

Tales Worth Retelling

stories from around the world

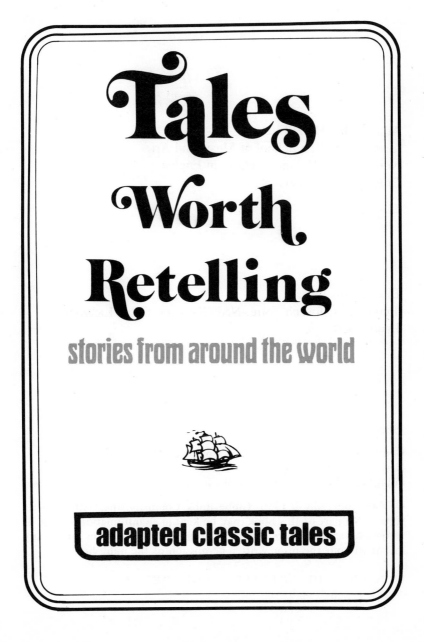

adapted classic tales

Adapted by: Herzl Fife
formerly of High School of Music and Art,
New York, N.Y., and Lecturer in English,
Columbia University

Illustrations by:
Tom Eaglin, Joseph Forté, Ned Glattauer, Oscar Liebman,
Lynda West

ISBN: 0-87065-047-5

PRINTED IN THE UNITED STATES OF AMERICA
1 2 3 4 5 6 7 8 9

iv

Adapter's Note

In preparing this edition of *Tales Worth Retelling,* the main purpose of each author has been kept in mind. Since the book was originally published, however, language has changed. We have modified or omitted some passages and some vocabulary. We have, however, kept as much of the original as possible.

Preface

The best reading is an adventure in imagination, the chance to be somebody else. In the pages to come, you are a bank manager in far-away India. You laugh the loud brutal laughter of ancient Rome. You see yourself plotting and planning for days—so that you can manage to repair a fine umbrella for nothing! Or you become a colonial governor, frightened by a strange ancient picture on the wall. Greed—greed may get you into the power of the devil. Or watch through that broken window pane—you will see a room in an Irish hut, and—

Reading is putting yourself into someone else's life for a while, acting new parts in new places. You learn as you do at a party or at games and contests. You learn because wonderful things are happening and you are part of them. Someone else's viewpoint, some trick you never knew, an unexpected kind of decency or honor—they surprise you by happening in your presence, and they stick in your mind. And here in a book you can hold the action a moment to think about it and to talk it over with others.

The stories in *Tales Worth Retelling* were written by many different authors. Originally they were longer and often more difficult. Someday you may want to read them in their complete form. Here they are shortened and altered so that you will find it easy to read each one in one session. Thus you may more clearly understand and remember the events, and find that discussing them is easy and pleasant. Enjoyment and understanding often travel together—a part of life that is called *education.*

Contents

A Germ Destroyer
Rudyard Kipling

Rudyard Kipling, British writer (1865-1936) You may know Kipling for his ballads, for his children's stories, or for his magic tales of India. He was born in Bombay and spent his youth in the country. After receiving his schooling in England, he returned to India and wrote verses, tales, and articles for Indian journals. He learned the point of view of the British soldier, of the government official, and of many kinds of natives. And yet he never lost the sense of mystery and adventure that visitors are more likely to feel in strange countries than are its inhabitants. He was a British writer of enormous popularity.

There was a time not long ago when England tried to rule India through a viceroy, a sort of minor king sent out to the city of Simla. With him went a secretary, who sometimes did more of the actual ruling than did the viceroy.

One of these secretaries was named John Fennil Wonder. He really was a wonder, too. He took just about everything off the shoulders of the viceroy. He made appointments, and interviewed people, and settled disputes. He could get all sorts of facts and figures together. He could do almost anything. And the viceroy, who was a very polite man, tried not to show his annoyance.

1

Wonder loved hard work, of course. But he tried to attend to things that were none of his business, and he went around making enemies. And the polite viceroy would watch him in a dreamy sort of way, and say, "My dear, good friend Wonder! When we all go to Heaven, I am sure he will try to steal Saint Peter's keys; or he'll get into a mess by pulling a feather out of Gabriel's wing. And then I shall simply *have* to report him!"

One season it happened that a visitor came to Simla, just to see the viceroy. He was a man with a single idea, an idea he could never forget, an idea that would improve the whole world, he was sure—and of course, an idea that made him a terrible nuisance. His name was Mellish. For 15 years he had studied the dreadful disease, cholera, in lower Bengal. He said that the germs flew through the damp air, and then stuck in the trees. But he had invented a heavy black-violet powder, "Mellish's Own Invincible Fumigatory.*" This powder, he insisted, would destroy all the germs of cholera.

He would talk loudly and beat the table with his fists. He would hide powders in his pockets and whip them out suddenly to wave under the noses of surprised people. He said that the surgeon general of India and all the hospital heads in the country were banded together into a medical ring, which was trying to hold back his invention. He wanted to get to the viceroy, to help him break this ring, and get the viceroy to understand his marvelous invention. And so Mellish came to Simla, and in his trunk were 84 pounds of "Mellish's Own Invincible Fumigatory."

Nobody, of course, would have given a cent for Mellish's chance to speak to the viceroy. It was simply impossible.

But there weren't so many hotels at Simla; and it so happened that there was another visitor in Simla—and his name was Mellishe—with an extra *e*. He was Mellishe of Madras, a very important government official who went around the country inspecting everything, and writing reports,

Fumigatory: disinfectant or pesticide.

and drawing a high salary. Everyone felt uncomfortable when he came around, and the highest government officials would always see him at once, so he would go on somewhere else and not bother them any longer. And the hotel where Mellishe of Madras stopped was the hotel of Mellish of Bengal.

The viceroy *had* to see Mellishe, as quickly as possible. So Wonder had to send out a quick note:

> Dear Mr. Mellish,
>   Can you set aside your other engagements and lunch with us at two tomorrow? His Excellency has an hour free at that time.
>   John Fennil Wonder

It was a very polite note; but you will notice that there was a blunder by Wonder. He had left off the *e* in *Mellishe*. The note, of course, was delivered to Mellish of the Fumigatory. Thus it was that before two the next day, Mellish, weeping with pride and delight, rode through the streets of Simla, with his pockets bulging with paper bags. What a wonderful chance! Just the viceroy and he at lunch—and all that marvelous black powder!

All through the lunch the inventor was restless. The viceroy was pleased with him because he did not talk about government business. He even offered his visitor a smoke. Smoke? At the word, Mellish spoke up like a man. He explained about cholera and his 15 years of labor. He told the viceroy *all* about the Simla ring, and how they opposed him and the Fumigatory. Soon Mellish's hair stood on end. Sweat broke out on his forehead. He stammered with excitement. He began poking at the pockets of his coat, bringing out the queerest paper bags.

The viceroy leaned back and watched the man through half-shut eyes. "I've caught the wrong kind of tiger, somehow," the viceroy told himself. "But this is a very *interesting* animal." And he awaited developments.

"J-j-judge for y-yourself, sir!" cried Mellish. "Y'Excellency shall judge for yourself!" And before anyone could stop him, he'd tipped a bagful of his powder into the silver ashtray, and plunged into it the lighted end of his cigar. The mess began to smoke like a volcano. Fat, greasy wreaths of copper-colored fumes went up. The room was filled with a sickening reek. Smoke took fierce hold on the windpipe and clamped down on it, and cut off all chance of breathing. The powder hissed and fizzed and sent out blue and green sparks into the murk, with the smoke billowing around them so it was impossible to see or breathe or gasp. Mellish was used to it. He enjoyed it; he seemed to thrive on it.

"Nitrate of strontia," he shouted. "Baryta! Bone meal! A cubic inch of the powder gives off a thousand cubic feet of smoke! Absolutely infallible! Not a germ could live in it for a minute—not a germ, Y'Excellency!"

By this time His Excellency had fled to the foot of the stairs, where he stood coughing. The place was humming with excitement, people running around trying to save the viceroy from a native attack, or an explosion of natural gases, or a general catastrophe. Red Lancers and macebearers rushed in, and ladies ran downstairs shrieking. "Fire!" All this did not improve the situation. Smoke began oozing out of the windows, and rolling across the halls in great storm clouds, and over-hanging the gardens.

Nobody could get to the center of the room where Mellish stood serene, still giving his lecture. The viceroy at the stairway said some wonderful things, but no one could hear him. And at last the horrible powder burnt itself out; and a courageous aide-de-camp rushed in and dragged out the lecturer. Mellish passed the viceroy in the hall, and began shaking a fresh bag of powder at him and telling of its virtues as he was dragged past. The viceroy could only stand there bent over with laughter. He waggled a feeble hand at the poor inventor and gasped,

"Glorious! Glorious! You are perfectly right! Not a germ—not a solitary germ could exist—I can swear it! A magnificent success!"

Through tears of laughter streaming from his eyes, His Excellency saw John Fennil Wonder come toward him. The secretary had seen the real Mellishe, it seemed, and—the viceroy waved away his Wonder, to finish his laugh in peace.

The story of all this made a number of people quite happy. There was first of all Mellish of the Fumigatory. He was perfectly sure he had at last broken the Simla medical ring, and that his life work had been recognized.

Next there was the viceroy. He could tell a story, when he wanted to. And he kept telling about "My dear good Wonder's friend with the powder." He told the story all over Simla. Wherever Wonder went he ran into people who knew this story, and they kept making little sly remarks to show that they knew it. It made Wonder feel quite uncomfortable, especially since the viceroy himself was always so greatly amused by it.

There was one afternoon, at a picnic, when the secretary sat just behind His Excellency, and simply had to hear every word that was said. It was that cursed story of Mellish again. But this time the viceroy added an ending that was new; he said it in such a harmless way that everyone in the group laughed heartily.

". . . and there was all this smoke whirling around us," said the viceroy, "and my dear, good Wonder was making his way through it. Why, I really thought for a moment that he had hired Mellish as a murderer, so that I would be put out of the way, and Wonder might become the next vice-roy. . . ."

The laughter showed it was all in good fun, of course. But Wonder knew that the viceroy wanted him to hear it. And he thought it over carefully, and wrote a letter saying that his health was not as good as it used to be, and perhaps he had better resign.

The viceroy thought that was a good idea too. He gave John Fennil Wonder a letter of the highest praise for his fine work as secretary.

A Bank Fraud
Rudyard Kipling

What a strange man to be guilty of a bank fraud—Reggie Burke! I don't think he'd like to have the story told; but he has left India now for Singapore, and there's little enough chance of his hearing it.

The *Sind and Sialkote Bank* it was. Reggie was manager of an up-country branch, far, far away from Bombay and Calcutta where the wise directors of the bank had their head-quarters. This area was a wheat province in upper India, where a bank manager needs a strong head and a touch of imagination if he is to turn out any sort of balance sheet. Care?—yes! Securities?—yes! But there's a good deal more to banking in such a region. One has to know when to take risks as well.

Reggie Burke knew just when to use the rules and when to put them aside. A practical fellow he was, with wide experience in native loan and insurance work. He knew the country and the natives thoroughly.

That kind of knowledge isn't gained in an office. There were two Burkes, really. Reggie Burke, between four P.M. and ten, was at your service for a polo game or drinking bout. It would take more than a gallon of Gunners' Madeira to make him stagger.

But between ten and four he was Mr. Reginald Burke,

Manager of the Sind and Sialkote Branch Bank. The greatest friendship on a polo field did not alter that a bit.

The bank directors pick their men carefully. They had tested Reggie under severe strains and trusted him as much as managers are ever trusted. His branch was a big one, with the usual staff: the manager—that was Reggie; one English accountant, a cashier, and a horde of clerks, besides the police patrol outside at night.

The business required that a clever manager get around among his clients a good deal and know quite a lot about their business. And this department was ably conducted by Reggie Burke, who taught many important things to Mr. Reginald Burke.

Now one day it was announced that a natural curiosity, a Mr. Silas Riley, was to be added to the bank staff as accountant. His father, as it happened, was a Member of Parliament. He owned a big block of stock in the bank. The son had weak lungs and might benefit from the hot climate in India.

Mr. Silas Riley himself had worked up to cashier in a bank, in the North of England, and had a great deal of experience in the factory districts. Of course, with such qualifications, it was clear to everyone who didn't know upper India that he ought to be placed as accountant in an up-country branch.

The new man proved to be a long, gawky Yorkshireman, full of pride and savage conceit. He was wonderfully narrow-minded in business and saw no difference between Indian banking and the regular, formal English sort.

His vanity was enormous. No one knew as much as he did about banking of any kind. In this he was strengthened by his letter of appointment. The usual polite phrases of such a letter seemed to him very special praise. He was being watched, he was sure, for brilliant achievements. He was to give special instruction to these poor, ignorant provincials and teach them their business.

When you add up his conceit, his narrowness, and the further facts of his physical weakness—the chest trouble I mentioned and his ill temper—you will admit that our bank manager should have regarded him as a natural curiosity—which he did.

But from the first day, Riley disapproved of Burke and had no hesitation about criticizing his manager. Reggie's pleasures appeared to Riley as offenses. His look of careless youth, the time he spent with boisterous army men, the wicked stories they told until Riley would leave the room—all these were a source of friction between the men.

Then there was also the fact that Mr. Riley found time to give Reggie frequent instructions on running his bank. Finally, Reggie had to remind him that seven years of experience in a factory district does not qualify a man for steering a great up-country business.

Local help has definite weaknesses. When a man's English assistant fails him, he has a hard task. Add to this the fact that as soon as winter began, Riley went sick with his lung trouble for weeks at a time. His work, of course, dumped itself upon his overworked superior.

Now, a traveling inspector for the bank discovered Riley's illnesses and reported them back to the directors. And meanwhile Mr. Riley's father, who was his only real backer at the bank, had died. Silas Riley himself knew nothing about his appointment and how it happened, so he had no understanding of the delicacy of his position.

Perhaps if Silas Riley had known why he was there, he might have acted better. But his illness alternated with stretches of persistent, active meddling, until Reggie could find relief only by inventing wonderful and hair-curling names for his assistant, after he had left him.

Reggie would stand clenching his fists and talking aloud to the air for minutes after the accountant was out of the place. But to Riley's face he was always polite, because, as he explained later, "Riley's such a frail beast that half of his loathsome conceit is due to pains in the chest." Then later in April, Riley went very sick indeed.

"Do you know how sick your accountant is?" the doctor asked Reggie.

"No!" said Reggie. "The worse the better, confound him. He's a clacking nuisance when he's well. You may walk away with the bank safe if you can just drug him silent for the hot weather."

"But I'm not joking," the doctor went on. "I'll give him another three months in his bed and a week or so more to die in. On my reputation, that's all the life he has left in the world. Consumption has hold of him to the marrow."

With that, Reggie changed into Mr. Reginald Burke. "What can I do?" he asked.

"Nothing. For all practical purposes the man is dead already. Keep him quiet and cheerful—that's all. I'll look after him to the end, of course."

The first letter Reggie opened that evening was from the directors. Mr. Riley was requested to resign within the month; official notice to him would follow, and the new accountant would arrive soon—a man Reggie knew and liked.

That letter was stowed away safely, and Reggie entered the sickroom to reassure his patient. Riley was as quarrelsome as ever. "With the way you run the bank, Mr. Burke, I don't see how we can get along in my illness," he complained.

The extra work his manager had to do in his absence he did not mention; but Riley made great talk about damage to his chances for advancement, because of this confounded illness. Reggie listened patiently, and assured him he'd consult with Riley daily on the management of the bank.

And long days crept through the big darkened house, while Reggie did the work of two men, and Riley stormed on his bed. The directors' letter dismissing Riley arrived. It was filed without being shown. The books, brought every evening to Riley's room, did not please the accountant. Everything possible was done to invent extra daily statements that would reassure him. By June, Riley was worried about the directors. Had they noticed his absence? Reggie said they had written sympathetic letters, hoping he could soon resume his valuable services.

"Sympathetic letters?" asked Riley. "Where are they? If they wanted to send sympathy, why didn't they send it to me? *You* don't need their sympathy, Mr. Burke—do you?"

Mr. Burke spent more time at his desk, finding just the right words for the directors to write to Mr. Riley. And a few days later Reggie opened Riley's mail for him in the half-lighted room, and offered him a letter without the envelope, from the directors.

"I will thank you not to interfere with my private papers," said Riley.

"I beg your pardon," answered Reggie. He had dropped tennis and polo to attend to his patient, but now he sat down to hear a tongue-lashing on the error of his ways—his horses, his liquor, and his bad friends.

"Of course, lying here on my back, Mr. Burke, I can't keep you straight. But when I'm well, I *do* hope you'll pay some heed to my words."

The arrival of Carron, the new accountant, was a great relief. It took some of the heavier duty off Reggie's shoulders and left him more time for forging complimentary letters from Calcutta. Of course, the new man's presence had to be explained to Riley. He was a friend, visiting Reggie—yes, that was it!

"You might have a little more consideration than to entertain your doubtful friends here at such a time," said Riley. So Carron slept at the club thereafter.

Meanwhile, of course, Riley's salary went on as usual. A check he wanted to send his mother went out in due form—out of Reggie's pocket. The thermometer was 116° in the shade, and the sick man sinking fast. The doctor looked at his patient a bit anxiously.

"He wants some sort of mental stimulant if he is to drag on. If you care for his living, keep him interested in life."

No sooner said than done. Somehow, against all the laws of business and finance, Riley received a 25 percent raise in salary from the directors. There was another letter of praise accompanying it. The trick succeeded so well that he lingered for another month, snarling and fretting about the bank, talking of the future, reading sermons on sin to Reggie from the Bible. . . .

At the end of September the heat was merciless. The evening was unbearable with the fierce, dusty air too strong for breathing. Reggie was sitting at Riley's bedside, when he saw the patient rise, gasping, "Mr. Burke, I am going to die. I know it myself. My chest is all hollow inside, and there is nothing to breathe with. To the best of my knowledge, I have done nought to lie heavy on my conscience. God be thanked, I have been preserved from the worse forms of sin. And I counsel *you*, Mr. Burke . . ." Reggie had to stoop lower to hear the rest.

". . . send my salary for September to my mother . . . done great things with the bank if I had been spared . . . mistaken policy . . . no fault of mine . . ."

With that he turned his face to the wall and died.

Reggie drew a sheet over the face and went out to the porch. A letter of condolence and sympathy for Riley, addressed from the directors, lay in his pocket, the last forgery of his bank fraud; his last "mental stimulant" was never to be used.

"If I'd been only ten minutes earlier," Reggie said to the stifling air around him, "I might have encouraged him to pull through another day."

A Terrible Night
Anton Chekhov

Anton Chekhov, Russian playright (1860–1904) *Anton Pavlovich Chekhov lived in the south of Russia. He was trained to be a doctor and got his degree M.D. at Moscow. He wrote a few short stories, which were printed and well received; and, when it became evident that Chekhov knew even more about the souls of people than he did about their bodies, he became a famous dramatist and short-story writer. His works show great variation, ranging from pathos to riotous farce.*

It was Christmas Eve in the year 1883. A wild night it was in Moscow. I don't know why I had to go to that awful spirit meeting! I don't believe in ghosts, or in spirits rapping on tables, or in any of that nonsense. Neither does my friend Restov, nor Godsacreov. But you know how friends are. "Come along, Requiemov," they urged. "We shall see how they do these things, and we'll have a good laugh afterwards!" So I went with them.

It was more impressive than I had expected. At first I was inclined to smile when I heard a voice come out of a saucer. But I was a little startled when it called my name. Even safe among my friends there, I felt uneasy!

"Requiemov! Your life is drawing to an end! Repent now," the voice said, with perfect plainness.

"I—I am not sure I heard," I said. "Will you repeat that, please?"

The saucer was very obliging. "Your life is drawing to an end *tonight*. Repent," it said distinctly. Well, the addition of a date did nothing to improve my spirits. I felt gloomy all through the rest of the meeting, especially when I remembered that my friends went home by different ways from mine.

My street lay in cold and darkness. There were no lamps to guide my footsteps. Rain was coming down in torrents. I was soon drenched to the skin and heartily sorry I had ever set out to our meeting or having set out, that I had not stayed the night with my friends. The wind howled overhead, not with the clear sound of an open place, but with the many voices of wind in the city—voices near and far, whistling across the house roofs, through trees, or across an open avenue, in different tones and pitches. But there was no human form to be seen anywhere on my trip, it seemed to me. The rain veiled all distances; and nearby there were only what looked like empty buildings; and the streets I trod were quite solitary.

"Your life is drawing to an end . . . repent now," the voice said with perfect plainness in my memory. All the unused streets of Moscow seemed to echo the words.

The voice sounded around every empty corner, more clear and convincing in the rain and wind than ever I had heard it from the saucer. A great dread seized me. I looked neither to right nor left, but hurried to my stairway and mounted to the fourth story without touching a single wall of.the hallway or brushing any doorpost or stairhead.

How dark it was, even when I had opened my door! How the wind moaned in the stove and rattled the ventilator!

"This is weird," I muttered. "If I can believe the voice, I must die tonight; and all this is a special dirge for my passing. But I cannot say that I am not fearful . . . ."

I scratched a match, just as the wind passed furiously over

my roof. The moaning became a roar, and a loose shutter swung with frantic blows against the outside wall, clattering its strange applause to the loud squealing of the ventilator, like a spirit in pain.

"It is something to have a house I can come to," I said in self-consolation. "There are many who haven't even such shelter."

Just then the match flared into a blue flame as I held it up to view the room. What a pity the wind had not extinguished it! The hair of my head moved. I shrieked with horror and despair and made for my door with both eyes shut tight.

There, in the center of my room, stood a coffin. It was unmistakable, even in a brief glimpse of terror. The cloth gleamed pink. There was a gold cross on the lid. It was a coffin evidently made for a young girl—the pink brocade, so fine in texture, the carved feet, the bronze handle—unquestionably for someone wealthy. With the image vivid before me, I ran from the room.

It is really surprising that I did not break my neck in my flight down the steps, my legs tangling in my long fur coat. If the floor or ceiling had fallen, or fire broken out—that was natural. But—this! Who would leave a coffin? Was there a corpse in it? I had not stayed to discover.

Perhaps it was brought there by some undertaker's error. Error indeed! When did an undertaker ever leave an expensive coffin without taking payment before he left the place? I leaned against a wet lamppost, where I stood drenched through, and muttered, "No. If it is not a miracle, then it must be some crime—some strange crime. The spirits foretold my death. Now they provide the coffin."

The absurdity of such a thought brought me back to some sense. The thing must have been an illusion, brought on by a trick in the placing of my furniture. I had never before observed it, until my nerves were overwrought with the meeting, the voice and the lonely walk in the rain.

The rain was still beating down, the wind penetrating. I had to find shelter. Well, maybe it *was* an illusion. But I certainly could not return to my room. That was out of the question. There was my friend Restov who lived a short journey away in Dead Lane, in the house of a merchant. Well, I resolved to find shelter at Restov's.

My friend was out, but the key was in its place on the door ledge. I went in gratefully, flinging my coat on the floor and groping for his sofa in the darkness. A cricket sang on the stove, and the Kremlin bells sang out for Christmas morning. My friend's room was much larger than mine and covered with some brown stuff that gave it a particularly gloomy look. But I held my lighted match up finally and looked around at this and that familiar object.

Why-y-y! What horror! I staggered from the room, nearly beside myself. There in full view stood a coffin! If this was an illusion my nerves must be diseased. Wherever I went I would always see this box of the dead horribly before me. I must be mad with some queer mania, caught when the spirit uttered his fearful words out of the saucer.

I could only seize my head in my hands and rock back and forth crying, "I must be going mad! Lord, what am I to do? I must be going mad!"

Outside, the rain still poured down on my feverish forehead. I was bareheaded, coatless; but on no account would I return to my room. Despair held me firmly. Even though I believed that I suffered from madness, the cold sweat stood out on my forehead, distinct from the rain, and mad as I seemed to myself, I could not help remembering that I might catch a dangerous cold standing in the rain.

There was my friend, Godsacreov, who lived not far off. He had been with us at the meeting. He lived in the fifth story of a fine house. Godsacreov was a physician. No doubt he could help me calm my nerves.

At the first step of his dwelling I heard a dreadful noise and someone slamming doors and running. "Help!" I heard.

"Help! Porter!" There was a dark figure rushing down the stairs toward me.

"Godsacreov! What's the matter? What ails you?" I managed.

He seized my hand as though I'd saved his life; he trembled and panted. "Is it really you, Requiemov—really you? You are pale—you are like a ghost—but no, it really is you, thank heaven!"

"But what's wrong with you?" I said. "You look like a ghost yourself."

"That blasted ghost meeting," panted my friend. "It's ruined my nerves so that I actually fancied—no, don't stare so. I know it's only my nerves—I actually thought I saw a *coffin* in my room upstairs."

I could not believe him, made him repeat it twice. Then, stammering and confused, I told him of the coffins *I* had seen.

When we were through staring at each other, we began pinching to see that we were not dreaming. Our tests were quite satisfactory and proved we were both wide awake. We did not suffer from illusions as I had fancied.

"What are we to do now, old man?" asked the doctor.

For a full hour we stood on the cold staircase making new guesses. When the cold became unbearable, we conquered our fear. "Porter! Porter!" we called, and made the man walk up before us and into the room. There we lit a candle. A fine coffin with white silver brocade and gold fringes and tassels rested there. Piously, the porter crossed himself.

"Is it—is it—vacant? Or inhabited?" asked the doctor. It took him quite a while to bend over the coffin and pull up the lid; I could see his face working all the while. No, it was not inhabited. It was quite empty, except for a letter inside that my friend read aloud.

Dear Godsacreov:
    You know how my father-in-law has got his business into a tangle—he's head over heels in debt. You know

that he's the best undertaker in town; but the creditors are taking over his goods tomorrow. They would like to take everything we own; ruin his family and mine. And our honor also would be lost. We had to find some way of hiding our goods from the creditors, or we were all lost.

Most of our property, you know, is in coffins. If we can only hide those for a while until this trouble blows over, we are saved. So we decided to hide our best coffins, sending one to each of our true friends. They can keep them in their rooms until they are called for. My dear old fellow, I assure you it is absolutely necessary and will save us from ruin. The coffin will remain with you for no more than a week, and then it will be called for.

To everyone whom I consider a true and sincere friend, I have sent a coffin, trusting in his nobility and kindness to hold it for us.

Affectionately yours,
Ivan Jawin

Well, our friend, the undertaker's son-in-law, saved his honor and his property I am happy to say. He is the owner of the business now and arranges funerals, sells monuments and gravestones, and so on.

For three months after that night I had to take a rest cure for jumpy nerves. And I am worried again now. Ivan's business isn't doing very well right now. And every evening I come home, and expect to find a white marble monument, or a gravestone, planted right next to my bedpost.

A Husk
Anton Chekhov

There is a little shed near the outskirts of the Russian village, Mironocitsk; it is often used by hunters as an overnight camp. Upon the hay just outside the doorway Ivan Ivanich, the veterinarian, rested one night. And inside, in the darkness, lay the schoolmaster, Burkin. They were relaxing after the day's hunting, and idly discussing the hermit, Marra. Marra was a perfectly healthy woman, quite normal. Yet she had never traveled even enough to see a town or railway. Sitting beside her stove all day—what a way to spend her life!

* * *

There's nothing wonderful in that, Burkin remarked. Take a schoolmaster who lived and taught with me until two months ago. This Bielikov was a teacher of Greek and a real hermit. It's just that some people seem to lack an instinct for companionship or a liking of common experience. He seemed to have no such instinct at all. He had drawn a shell, or husk around himself, to protect him from the world, and this extended to the least detail of his life.

Why, for example, did we always see him, even on the dryest days, carrying an umbrella sheathed in its case and wearing galoshes on his feet? Why was his watch pulled out of a small case whenever he glanced at it—or even his pocketknife drawn from a little holder whenever he wanted to sharpen a pencil?

If he took a cab, he would put the hood down. His ears were stuffed with cotton. Even his mind sought things dead and completed that would not disturb him with difficult problems and consequences. That, no doubt, was why Greek was his subject.

"Ah, how sonorous is the Greek tongue! How beautiful!" he would say. Then he would raise a finger for attention; a rapt look came upon his face, and he would prove his point by pronouncing with the drollest possible expression, "Anthropos!*"

His mannerisms, his thoughts, his actions—in everything he found special *limits.* Something forbidden, a circular forbidding teachers to be on the streets after nine P.M.—that appealed to him. It was something fine—and definite! But something new, or unclear, or positive—a reading circle, or a new dramatic club—"well, they are all right, of course, most excellent—but—but what will come of it?" he asked doubtfully.

This prudence and fear of rule-breaking extended to everyone. A teacher late for services, an instructress seen walking late with an army officer, would set his tongue wagging. "What will come of it?"

And our teachers' meetings were sadly browbeaten by his insistence on the letter of every law. We were actually afraid to pass a student he disapproved of—what would he think or say about *us* if we did? His black-rimmed eyeglasses, his little white face staring at us—his presence was oppressive. His influence affected everything.

It was a rule that teachers must keep on good terms with their colleagues. So it became Bielikov's habit to walk into our rooms and sit there for several hours without uttering a word. He liked it as little as we did—but after all, it was his duty! The director himself feared him. For 15 years the

*Anthropos: Greek word meaning human.

school went cautiously for fear of displeasing him. Towns-
women feared to organize their theatricals for fear of his dis-
approval. Teachers feared to make friends, read books, help
the poor, teach enthusiastically.

Bielikov lived next door to me, Burkin continued, ignoring an interruption from his companion outside the hut. There
were shutters and locks to protect him. A half-witted soldier,
Athanasius, cooked for him, because he would not keep a
female servant. The room was always hot; but Bielikov slept
under the bedclothes, shivering with fear and apprehension.

And yet—would you believe it?—this empty shell, this
husk of a man, was nearly married once.

Here Ivan knocked the ashes from his pipe and peered in
at the doorway toward the schoolmaster. "You're joking!"
he said, incredulous. But inside the hut, the schoolmaster
only talked on placidly.

No, I am not. Michael Kovalenko, a Ukrainian, was appointed to teach history and geography at our school. He
brought his sister Varinka with him. She was about thirty,
well-built and healthy, jolly, always singing or roaring with
laughter. And he was a big strapping fellow, too. On the
director's birthday, we were going to have our usual deadly
gathering of bored teachers—but Varinka upset the apple cart.
She sang her Ukrainian songs, joked, laughed, and had us all
entranced—even Bielikov! He began smiling sweetly, and he
suddenly remarked very loudly:

"The Ukrainian accents, by their tenderness and soft
harmonies, are very much like the sounds of ancient Greek."

Somehow this seemed to please and flatter the young
woman. She talked to him about the farm she owned, about
pumpkins and watermelons, and the tasty Ukrainian *borsht*.
As we all listened, the same thought swept our circle—why not
let Bielikov marry her? The director's wife whispered it to
me; for the first time we remembered that this strange man
was unmarried. And to everyone at once it seemed most de-
sirable to correct that condition.

Boredom encouraged the idea. Never was a party given, but the teacher of Greek and Varinka were pointedly invited— together. There was the strong influence of widespread public opinion and constant suggestion; and besides that, there was the fact that Varinka and her brother, in their hearty vigorous way, were always quarreling, even quite publicly on the streets. And no doubt it was high time she had a home of her own and could go her ways without explaining them.

It was not so very strange, then, that Varinka showed some interest in Bielikov. She would sing for him, or they would go walking. Very often we could hear her laughter ringing out when she was in his company. She was pleasing to look at, well-born, not poor. Beilikov kept her photograph on his table and reflected very seriously. The effect on him was not good; for he grew even paler and thinner with doubt.

"Marriage is a fine thing. But this came up so suddenly. Where will it all lead to?" he would say to me.

"Stop worrying," I told him. "Just marry and be done with it!"

"No, no! It's a serious matter. Something unforeseen might happen. Both she and her brother are bold characters— odd ways of thinking." And he considered every obligation and responsibility but he did not propose. The women of the town were growing angry and impatient.

Despite all that, he might have married; but a great scandal arose suddenly.

Michael Kovalenko, Varinka's brother, loathed Bielikov, of course. He called him a spy and hurled contempt at the whole town for taking him so seriously.

"I'll stay here a little longer," Kovalenko said. "Then I'll go back to my farm and catch crabs and teach the Ukrainians. You can stay here with your little Judas."

Or else he would laugh at one of Bielikov's long and melancholy visits. "If Varinka wants to marry that spider, why all right," he would say. "But she might as well marry a lizard."

And one day someone drew a fine caricature of Bielikov in galoshes and homespun trousers, walking arm in arm with Varinka, his umbrella open above them. The resemblance was remarkable. And below was inscribed, "The enamored anthropos." Every teacher and official, including Bielikov, received a copy.

Now on that same day, we were all to go for a walk in the woods, both teachers and pupils. Bielikov's lip quivered, and he began talking about the wickedness of mankind. Just then Kovalenko came up on a bicycle, with Varinka on another behind him. They threw us a cheerful greeting and rode on ahead. Poor Bielikov turned green and then white; "Women—and school-teachers! Riding bicycles!" he gasped.

"What's wrong with that? It's good for the health," I said. But he was past listening. He went back home at once, unable to go any further with us.

Next day I noticed he was shivering and nervous, ate nothing, and even in the intense heat wore his warmest clothes. And that evening he called on Kovalenko.

Michael happened to be in a surly mood and was quite short with the fellow. What did he mean by objecting to such a harmless thing? Why not mind his own business?—and so on. Bielikov's pained attempts to explain his position only infuriated his host, who very quickly wished him good speed to the devil. At this Bielikov demanded that he respect authority. Kovalenko demanded, "Whose authority?" and said he did not care to converse with a spy.

This was too much. Bielikov said he must report the whole conversation to the school officials, because somebody might have overheard it, and might report it inaccurately. And in appreciation of this little gem of tactfulness, Kovalenko kicked his visitor down the stairs.

There was no physical injury. But Varinka came in just then, and seeing her suitor in the act of picking himself up from the landing, she laughed loud and long. And that laughter seems to have ended the hope of Bielikov's marriage and even his existence on this earth.

After that he could not seem to understand anything Varinka said to him, even with the best intentions. He simply went to his room, removed her photograph and went to bed. Three days later his poor half-witted servant Athanasius came to me for help. Bielikov lay in bed quite still, hidden by covers and even curtains. His only answers to my questions and remarks were "Yes" and "No." Athanasius frowned and sighed for a few days, and walked around smelling of vodka like a tavern.

Then at the end of a month Bielikov died. The whole school attended his funeral; and I must say that for the first time he now seemed contented. For one thing, it happened to be a rainy day, and we all came to him wearing galoshes and walked with our umbrellas open. He had reached his ideal at last; he was going to be placed in a protecting case from whence he should never be taken. Varinka was there too. She cried a little when the coffin was lowered.

I think most of us returned from the funeral relieved and free, like children left to play in the house, with their elders away for the day.

But in a week or so, we found our lives just as stagnant even without the circulars and talebearing. The same bonds were on us too, I suppose, though not so plainly in sight. How many there are. . .! How many there will be. . .!

* * *

The schoolmaster, Burkin, walked out of the shed into the moonlight, and he looked across to the village street, at the cottages, the haystacks and the slumbering willows. To the left, where the houses stopped, a wide field extended, perfectly silent, bathed in moonlight, without sound or motion upon it.

"Time to turn in," remarked Burkin.

But the veterinarian, Ivan, was muttering to himself, staring across the field. "To listen to them telling lies, and call you a fool for letting them. To be too cowardly to speak out for honesty and freedom, but lie there and smile . . . for a crust of bread, a little warmth, or some useless decoration . . . Such a life! Such a life is impossible!"

In ten minutes Burkin was asleep. Ivan Ivanitch still smoked his pipe in the doorway, sending up the short, angry puffs that showed how deeply he was disturbed.

The Bet
Anton Chekhov

"Capital punishment! Why, it's a holdover of the dark
ages," someone was saying. It was a party of clever and
learned men at the house of a young banker. Their host had
a lively discussion on his hands as soon as his guests began
talking about the death penalty.

"I'm sorry I can't agree with you," the banker cut in.
"Of course, I myself can't claim to have suffered the death
penalty, nor even solitary confinement. But judging entirely
from reason, condemning a man to death seems a thousand
times better and more humane than life imprisonment, alone
and solitary. Why, surely, an executioner who kills you at
one stroke must be more kind than one who draws your life
out in a perpetual agony of wasting years—."

"No! No! They are both abominable," one of the guests
insisted. "To take away a life—who should take life but the
Lord? How shall the State take the divine power and destroy
what it cannot restore? The State is not God; let it not tam-
per with human life, then!"

Here a young lawyer put in his voice. "No doubt you
are right," he said, as if he were turning the matter over in
his mind patiently. "They are perhaps both without justice.
But if I had the choice, I know very well it is better to live
on any terms than to die altogether. Even solitary confinement would be better than death. . . ."

"Nonsense!"

"Ridiculous!"

"Of course it's so!"

"No one wants to die!"

Half a dozen voices jumped at the statement, until the host, the banker, rapped the table for a hearing.

"It is flatly untrue—a stupid lie, I tell you! Two million rubles—I'll bet two million rubles that you yourself won't stand solitary confinement for five years! A lifetime! Bah!"

"If you mean that," said the lawyer, "I'll take up your bet. Not only 5 years—but 15 years; I will remain in solitary confinement for 15 years, and receive from you the two million rubles!"

"Fifteen! Fifteen!" cried the banker, as though he had just swung a deal. "I accept. Gentlemen, be my witnesses— I stake two million, against 15 years of his liberty!"

It was a cruel, useless bet. Many of the guests tried to get them to cancel it. But the banker was delighted. He had just gained a great deal of wealth on recent business—a few million rubles were nothing! Why, he could hardly count up all his money! All through the supper he kept reminding the young lawyer that he was acting like a fool.

"Well, have you thought better of it?" he'd call across. "Two millions are nothing to me—but three or four years of the best part of your life are something to consider! That's right—three or four, I said. You'll never last beyond that, I can tell you, and they'll simply be wasted. Not a cent is yours if you leave beforehand. Why, the very fact that you can walk out of the place any minute you choose will be like poison to you. You'll never be able to stand the constant temptation. . . ."

In an abandoned building on the banker's grounds, the "prison" was arranged. For 15 years the lawyer must not cross over its threshold, nor see any human being, nor hear the voice of anyone. Neither could he receive letters nor newspapers. Musical instruments and books of all sorts were permitted him, wine, and smoking tobacco. With the outer world, his only communication must be in silence, through a glass window. Any quantity of the things permitted, he could order. He must pass his order note through the window to a guard on duty. The smallest details of this wager were discussed and settled. At 12 o'clock on November 14, 1870, the confinement began: to last until 12 o'clock, November 14, 1885. The slightest attempt on the part of the lawyer to violate the least obligation under their agreement meant that he lost his wager.

For the first year the lawyer suffered greatly from boredom. Wine he let alone; tobacco he would not have either. Light novels, with complicated, fantastic plots, he read by the dozen. By the second year the sounds of the piano, once heard frequently, ceased altogether. Great books of classical literature became his reading.

But in the fifth year, the music resumed, and he asked for wine. Guards who peered through his window saw him pacing the room or casting himself on the bed to weep bitterly, utterly desolate and forlorn. Such moods were often followed by fits of yawning or raging anger. He would write for hours and then in frenzy rip his work into a thousand pieces.

The time that followed saw him hard at work, reading great books of philosophy and history, or deep in the study of language. Over 600 volumes were sent him in the next few years, written in many languages. One day he sent his jailer a letter written in six languages, with the request that a gun be fired in the garden, if there was no error in any of the letters.

And the gun was fired! Genius seemed to have flared up in the prisoner and burned steadily and unremittingly in him— a genius for intellectual labor.

More than ten years after the man's imprisonment, a copy of the New Testament was sent him. And for a whole year, day after day, hour after hour he sat at his desk, poring over the single slim volume. Then, religion ... theology ... no branch of literature confined him, yet all floated about him . . . chemistry . . . poetry . . . medicine . . . a sea of words seemed at last to surround him.

Now, at 12 o'clock on the night of November 13, 1885, the night before the prisoner's release, the banker paced his study, pausing only to stare into the dark autumn that pressed against his windows. "I shall be a ruined man tomorrow," he said. "To satisfy the bet, I must pay him two million rubles. What remains? With the payment of two million rubles, I shall be bankrupt."

It was true. Fifteen years had seen his decline. Bad risks had reduced his fortune, so that every wind that tossed the markets of the world drew groans and trembling from him, fears that overwhelmed him.

"A wager? It was not a wager! It was a suicide pact! The man is going to destroy me," he said. "Only 40 years old! Why, he will take my money only to laugh in my face. I shall give him everything I have and he will mock my poverty! I must be a beggar—only to envy his prosperity!

"'No! No! I owe it all to you, my friend; let me help you,' he will say." And this thought was worse than the thought of poverty to the banker.

"A man cannot bear it! Ruin and shame! I must escape— even if he dies for it . . . even if he dies for it!" As the clock struck three, frozen leaves answered the night winds. A dark cold rain swept the garden, pouring itself in streams from the tree branches. Silently, he swung his safe door open and he slipped the key, rusted with 15 years of idleness, into his over-coat. The house of the prisoner lay quiet under the rain, and no step stirred.

"Ivan! Ivan!" called the banker. The watchman did not answer. He must be sleeping. . . .

"Now if I only have the courage! Ivan will be blamed," the banker answered himself softly. No one at the door . . . in the lobby . . . at the stairway . . . now, across the grounds . . . only the flare of his match, held to the prisoner's keyhold. There sat the lawyer at the table, slouched over a paper, motionless. No response to a faint tapping at the door frame. The rusty lock creaked hoarsely and the door squeaked as the banker entered.

Surprise? Alarm? Resistance? No sound greeted his advancing footsteps, nor his clenched, poised hand. Yes, there was the prisoner, like some skinny skeleton, covered with long matted hair and shaggy unkempt beard, the face yellow with the color of earth in the hollow cheeks, the earth from which it came—so soon to return there. What a frightful hand over that page, an image of death, not the figure of a man only 40 years of age, seated asleep at his table. Yet it was only sleep that held the prisoner still, sleep that sprawled the skeleton finger out over the page, to point at the painfully written words that lay there—a page for a murderer!

The banker moved dry lips. "Wretched! Wretched! I could smother this single spark with a pillow. No one could see." The banker's eye dropped to the paper and traced its writing. Softly, he removed the pointing finger that concealed some of the words there.

"Tomorrow, at noon, I have my freedom. What a mockery that is, to gain my freedom, now that I have learned well to despise it. For 15 years I have known your world better than one who lived in it. In books I have drunk your wines, hunted your deer, loved women. I have heard the night winds whisper tales of wonder, seen the sun over Mont Blanc, and the sunset staining sky and ocean with purple. Demons have spoken to me of God. Words have brought me wonder and wisdom. To what purpose? That a profound contempt should fill my being for the habits of your world—the worthless, false, empty, deceptive things valued by men. Death comes to your genius. Your history, your heirs, your wisdom, they are no more than the story of mice that die under your floors. Falsehood seems to you true. Ugliness seems like beauty. Like frogs and lizards that might have grown about your fruit trees, like the fragrance of sweating horses breathing from your roses—so have you exchanged the worth of heaven for earth. Is not that contemptible? Notice how deeply I believe this.

"Tomorrow I should receive two million rubles for this imprisonment. But I shall forfeit them—renounce them! Five hours before the hour appointed by our bet, I shall leave my prison and break the terms of our contract. Nothing—nothing will be owing to me."

For a while the banker could hardly believe his eyes. A red shame washed over his features as he kissed the strange creature before him and crept from the house in silence. All the night, tears of remorse and thankfulness kept him awake. Then, in the morning, watchmen came to him to say that the prisoner had crept through a window into the garden, whence he had escaped. The banker descended to the garden and saw it was so. But the prisoner's paper, which he found on the desk in due order, the banker carried carefully home with him; and he locked it into his safe so that no idle talk might disgrace his share of the bet.

The Upper Berth

F. Marion Crawford

Francis Marion Crawford, American Novelist (1854–1909) Mr. Crawford might well be called a citizen of the world. Born in Italy of American parents, he was educated in New England. From there he emigrated to India, and became editor of a newspaper. He was fascinated by the study of the ancient Sanskrit language and mastered many other languages as well. His immense production of novels made them each little "pocket theaters," swiftly written and carelessly plotted. Hidden wills, forgeries, and disguises keep popping out of his quick-paced plots.

Mr. Brisbane was a powerful man, about 35, over six feet tall, with big hands and a massive chest. He had often made trips across the Atlantic. On one voyage he had cabin 105, lower berth, on a boat called the *Kamtschatka.*

When Robert, the steward, came up, Mr. Brisbane directed him to take his bags to 105. The man picked up the bags; but there was an odd, strained look on his face. He muttered something under his breath which made Brisbane think he must be a little drunk. Nevertheless, Brisbane followed him up to his cabin.

Cabin 105 was a big double room, he found, furnished

with blankets, a sink, and a toothbrush rack about the size of an umbrella stand. Over Brisbane's lower berth was another, its drab curtains half closed. This was vacant when he came in.

He spent a lazy day on deck, just loafing about, and thinking idly of the steward's haste to get out of the cabin; and he decided to turn in early. Then he found that someone was sharing the room with him. The luggage was all there already; and not long afterward the stranger came in, a pale, sandy-haired fellow, who looked as if he'd rather not be spoken to. Brisbane took one good look and decided to avoid the fellow—though he needn't have bothered, really. He was never to see him again.

During the night a thud came from the upper berth to the floor, as though the stranger had leaped clear out of bed. There was frantic fumbling at the door-bolt and sounds of the man rushing madly down the passage, leaving the door wide open behind him. The boat was rolling heavily, and the door slammed to and fro in the darkness.

Brisbane got up, swearing, and shut the door before turning in again. But his sleep was restless. Before dawn he awoke, finding the cabin damp and ghastly cold, with the smell of sea water all through it; and he heard someone turn over and groan in the berth above him before he dropped off to sleep again.

In the morning, it was still amazingly cold for a June day. The ship still rolled, and the porthole was wide open, with the lid hooked back. The stranger in the upper berth must have been cold too, for the curtains were drawn close together. Though the damp sea smell was gone now, the place was uncomfortable enough. Brisbane decided to take a turn on deck; so he shut the porthole impatiently and hurried above.

There he found that the day was not cold at all, as the cabin had been, but warm and cloudy, with an oily swell over the water. The ship's doctor was there too, a tremendous Irishman, with black hair, blue eyes, and a hearty, healthy look about him.

"Clear enough out here," Brisbane remarked. "You'd never know my cabin was so damp!"

"Damp?" the doctor asked, surprised. "Whereabouts are you?"

"One hundred and five," Brisbane answered. The doctor started and simply stared at him. "You aren't the only one to complain about that cabin," he told him.

The doctor seemed especially interested in the events of the night, the stranger in the upper berth, and his mad scamper down the passage during the night. "Look here," he broke in finally, "what do you say to sharing my cabin with me—and well, just move right out of number 105!" Brisbane declined the offer, a bit airily, and went on talking about the porthole, left open so annoyingly in the night.

The doctor faced Brisbane with a most serious expression. "I would rather see a man overboard then occupying cabin 105," he said emphatically. "In fact—the last three occupants actually did jump overboard!"

The big man shook hands with the doctor, searching his face for any sign of spoofing; but there wasn't any. Again he declined to stay with the doctor, politely, and said he had no intention of jumping overboard. Calmly, he went up to breakfast.

People at the tables seemed unusually grave; and soon afterward, Robert, his steward, came to tell him that the captain wanted to speak to him.

"Your roommate has disappeared," the captain told him simply. "Was there anything queer about his actions?"

Well, that was just about the limit, coming after the doctor's warning. The man was probably overboard; he seemed to be nowhere on the ship. And that made the fourth passenger who had gone overboard from room 105, as Brisbane remarked to the captain. The captain was pretty angry to hear that this story was generally known; but he told Brisbane that two of the other three had done the same thing. Each had dashed down the passage in the night, as their roommates told it, and had gone right over the rail, in full sight of the watch.

This was too much for the captain; he had the reputation of the ship to consider. And he warned Brisbane, for his own safety, to move his belongings into another cabin, even into the captain's if he desired it. Only he must remain silent on shipboard about the little drama of the morning.

Brisbane agreed that this was a fair bargain, but the mystery seemed clear enough, he said. The cabin was damp; the porthole had been left open. The stranger, no doubt, had caught a chill, and had jumped over in delirium. At any rate, he repeated, he had no intention of doing the same; and with the captain's leave, he would remain where he was for the voyage!

"It's your own affair," the captain told him seriously. "But I think you're being foolish." And later, on deck again, the ship's doctor met him and told him the same.

No one, even if he is not superstitious, could have been really as cool as Brisbane pretended to be. He himself admitted that after a long evening of cards, when he went back to his stateroom, he kept thinking of the tall stranger, drowned and tossing about in the long swell or three hundred miles astern. He even looked into the empty upper berth to make sure the man was not there. Then the cabin air seemed cold again; and turning about he saw that the porthole was once more open and carefully fastened back!

That was the last straw! Brisbane summoned the steward and bawled him out furiously. The poor fellow, scared enough, insisted that no one could keep that porthole closed; and he even bet a gold coin that if he did shut it—it would be opened again and fastened back securely, in half an hour!

Brisbane inspected the great screw, now fastened down, and the looped nut that ran through it; and he promised to pay Robert his gold coin, if it were again found open.

For about five minutes that evening, Brisbane lay in the cabin. The dim corridor light filtered in through the ground glass panel of his room door. Soon that light too was lowered, and he stared at the porthole in the darkness. Nothing moved. For a whole hour of waiting and staring, nothing moved.

Then, as he had barely relaxed into dozing, there was a draft of cold air. Sea spray blew through the room; and as he rose to his feet, the violent motion of the ship hurled him across the stateroom. The porthole was wide open again; and as he felt for the catch, he found it was fastened back—open! The brass fittings were heavy and hard to move. It could never have been shaken open by accident—and besides, it was fastened back!

He closed it at once, and with all his great strength, screwed down the loop nut, staring the while with eyes now wide awake at the sea foam, streaking white and grey past the thick glass. Something seemed to move in the upper berth behind him. When he turned to look, there was nothing visible, but he heard a faint groan. At that he sprang across the room, tore aside the curtain, and thrust in a hand. There *was* someone there.

As the curtain parted, a gust of wind came forth that smelled horribly of stale sea water. Something smooth, wet and icy cold lay within. As he tugged at it, a clammy mass, heavy and wet, sprang out, hurling him across the room; in an instant the door was open and the thing rushed forth. Brisbane heard it dash ahead down the dim passage, ten yards or so before him. Then the corridor was silent, leaving him in frank terror, holding to the polished rail at a turn in the passage.

Returning badly shaken, he found that the whole cabin smelled of stagnant sea water, and a creeping horror came over him as he saw the porthole. Again it was wide open—and latched back, as he had first seen it!

He took a light and examined the upper berth, expecting to find it wet with sea water. But though the berth had evidently been slept in, it was now perfectly dry.

There was no sleep that night for the traveler.

Through the brass loop in the mysterious porthole he thrust a heavy stick. With that as a lever, he wrenched the plate shut till the heavy metal bent under the pressure. For the rest of the night he sat under a lighted reading lamp, staring in bewilderment until dawn.

In the morning he told the events of the night to the ship's doctor. "You seem to think I am likely to doubt the story," the doctor said smiling. "I do not doubt it in the least. I renew my invitation to you. Bring your bags here and take half my cabin."

Brisbane was resolved to get to the bottom of the matter. "It has no bottom," said the doctor. "It will never be explained in nature!" But the ship's captain felt as Brisbane did—there must be some way to discover it. And Brisbane and the captain, therefore, prepared to spend the night in 105.

Carpentry was carefully examined for loose boards or panels. Planks were tried, flooring tapped, and the hardware taken out and refitted. Then the carpenter spoke up as a plain man. "A half-dozen four-inch screws through the cabin door," he said. " 'Twere the best way to deal with *this* mystery!"

But courage runs higher by day then by night; and Brisbane went ahead and arranged to keep watch that night with the captain in room 105, that had seen four passengers mysteriously destroyed.

The captain was a comfortable man to have along on such a venture. He was calm, self-possessed, not at all the sort that would yield to superstition. He put a heavy suitcase before the door, to sit on; and they searched the cabin together to be sure it was vacant. "It is impossible for any human being to get in, or to open the porthole," Brisbane observed.

"Very good," said the captain. "If we see anything now, it is either our imagination, or something not human." And he settled back comfortably in a chair.

"The first time things happened was in March," he said.

"The man who slept in this upper berth turned out to have been a lunatic, and he had taken his passage without the knowledge of his relatives. He rushed out in the middle of the night, and he threw himself overboard before the officer of the watch could stop him. On the very next trip—Why, what are you looking at?" he demanded suddenly.

Brisbane's eyes were on the porthole, where the brass loopnut was beginning to turn slowly—very slowly—barely visibly, on the screw. He rose and tried it. It was plainly loosened.

"The second man went through this port," the captain whispered. And now a dank odor of stagnant water was plain. The reading lamp flickered a moment and died down. There was only the diffused passage light glowing through the glass panel in the darkness.

The ship rolled heavily, and the curtain of the upper berth rose and fell. At the same time the captain went swiftly to wrestle with the brass loop of the port. But it turned against his strong hands. Brisbane thrust his heavy oak stick through the ring, straining against it. In a moment, the cane had snapped. He was hurled backward, and the port was open.

"There is something in the berth!" the captain cried, staring horribly. Brisbane leaped for it, and his hands seized something. It was like the body of a man long drowned, yet it moved with the strength of ten living men. The putrid smell of sea water was all about it, and shiny hair hung in foul wet curls over the dead face. Quickly it forced the man back, winding sinewy arms around his neck until he fell, overpowered. The captain struck hard at it; but he soon fell forward with a cry.

The thing seemed to pause a moment, hovering over the fallen captain. Then it moved, to vanish through the open porthole. Brisbane found that his arm was broken. As for the captain, he was badly stunned, and he swore never to sail again on that vessel.

But the ship's carpenter won his point after all, for six

four-inch screws were run through the door of cabin 105. And when any passenger asks for a berth in that stateroom, he is told that it is taken. And it is taken—by a ghost!

In all other ways, the *Kamtschatka* runs well enough. With its cabin 105 boarded up, it acts exactly like any other vessel.

The Umbrella

Guy de Maupassant

*Guy de Maupassant, French short-story writer (1850–
1893)   There are few short-story writers who have
de Maupassant's ease in drawing characters swiftly and
firmly.   Where other writers might require many details,
de Maupassant uses only a few, with great power of suggestion.   In his youth he had been a clerk and a soldier,
but the famous French novelist Flaubert was his god-
father and helped him develop his remarkable powers in
the short story.   His brief, realistic short stories, often
having a surprise ending, have had tremendous influence
on story writers everywhere.*

"Why, we're not even living up to our income! Surely
we could spend a little more. What is the use of earning
money, if we must always put it by, even going without things
we need?"

It was the little M. Oreille speaking to his wife. One of the
head clerks at the Parisian War Office, he remained in his job
simply because his wife insisted. Their income outside of his
work was sufficient, but she would not hear of cutting off a
franc.   She was a woman about 40, bustling, sharp in her
words, scrupulously clean, and with a perfectly furious
temper.

What rash forgetfulness had induced him to speak to her so? Surely no one understood it better than he. Well, tonight he was lucky. Her temper was calm at the moment.

"It is better to have too much than too little," she answered quietly. "You never can tell what may happen. If I were more generous with our money, we could not be so safe."

But, for all his good fortune in the argument with Mme. Oreille, I am afraid M. Oreille was not content. You see, for two years he had been going around with an ancient, patched umbrella, that was the standing joke of his office. And when, by a heroic attack against his wife's thriftiness, he had induced the lady to get him a new umbrella—why, it was the eight-and-a-half-francs kind, on display at every cheap department store. Such umbrellas marked the lower orders of humanity on every street in Paris—a cheap umbrella, a shoddy, homely clumsy umbrella.

But the War Office staff found it an excellent umbrella indeed. M. Oreille's coworkers immortalized it in song and story. They told jokes about it that were quite true, and invented others that weren't. They roared ballads about it that shook the rafters and made more thunder than those paper cannon did, that their pens were always scratching about.

M. Oreille was very angry. He *demanded* a new umbrella, to be made of good silk, to cost no less than 20 francs—and he must see the receipt for the umbrella, to prove that his wife had paid that price. Well, would you believe it? Mme. Oreille really did buy him a new umbrella. The receipt she handed him said 18 francs, and her face was red with anger at the trouble she expected.

"This will last you for no less than five years," she said.

I wish you could have seen Oreille at the office. An entirely new subject had to be discovered for the jokes and ballads. The new umbrella was pronounced perfectly respectable. How he flourished it, walking homeward! A sense of security and power possessed him that was quite gratifying.

You must surely know, however, that all happiness based

upon material things is fleeting. In this instance, M. Oreille came home, and his wife took the umbrella from his hand.

"The elastic must never be so tight," she said with a worried look. "It will cut into the silk." And she shook the folds out to refresh them, lest they be pinched to an early death. But horror held her hand. There, in the middle of one fold, was a cigar burn, bigger than even a farthing.

"Why, you—you——you've burnt your new umbrella. Burnt a hole right through it! Why, you must be mad—trying to ruin us completely—"

The sense of power was quite gone now; he grew pale. "What's that? What did you say?"

"Look here!—here—burnt your umbrella!" For a moment she seemed about to beat him with it; but she only shook it under his nose.

"I just opened it once to show to the others at the office," he said. "That's all I did with it except carry it!"

That was just the beginning, of course. The rest of the evening was consumed in one of those stormy scenes about which the less said the better. She patched the hole with part of the old umbrella, which was of a different color. Next day Oreille thrust the mended article into his locker at the office, glad to forget it for the day.

Well, that evening Mme. Oreille went straight for the umbrella and checked on its condition. It was ghastly. Evidently someone had emptied a lighted pipe over it in the locker; it was riddled with burn holes, ruined beyond the possibility of use. Oreille was too stunned to speak, his wife, too enraged. They stared at it dumbly together. Her arm was able to move before her lips, so she threw the umbrella at his face.

"You—you scoundrel! You unspeakable rascal! You did it on purpose—but I'll pay you back! You'll never get another . . ."

It was a good hour before he was able to state that he knew nothing of the damage, that it probably had been done for spite or for revenge. Then a friend arrived who was to

dine with them, and he heard the case through as Mme. Oreille told it. A real friend he was, too.

"If you do not buy a new umbrella, or repair this one," he said, "M. Oreille will spoil much more valuable clothes in the rain. Better think it over."

"Never. It will cost eight francs at least to re-cover it! Eighteen francs for the umbrella! Why, that would be 26 francs for an umbrella! For an umbrella! It's madness! It's idiocy!"

"Look here," said the calm visitor. He was a poor man himself, and knew a few things. "Your fire insurance company will pay you for any damage by burning, if it is done in your house. Now in this case . . . ."

"Tomorrow morning," said Mme. Oreille with decision, "before going to the office you will stop at the Maternelle Insurance office, show the damage and make your claim."

M. Oreille showed admirable firmness. "I'll do no such thing," he said. "We have a loss of 18 francs, and that's the end of it." And next morning he carried a stick. Fortunately, the weather was fine.

Mme. Oreille left the umbrella on the table, and spent the

morning looking at it. In public she was timid, blushed at a word, and was afraid of strangers. The thought of facing the challenging glances of the insurance people frightened her nearly as much as the loss of her money—but not quite!

When it was close to afternoon, she took a match and burnt a hole as big as her fist in the remaining covering. Then she daintily rolled up the wreck, and marched to the Rue de Rivoli. Ah, yes—twenty-eight numbers more to the insurance office—time to think it over still. . . . There it was! "La Maternelle Fire Insurance," plain as day over the door.

Past the entrance, a maze of wire cages, each housing a clerk deep in his tasks—hmmm!—there, that gentleman with the sheaf of papers in his hand would know. . . .

"Excuse me, Sir, but could you direct me to the department of claims for burnt property?"

"First floor to the left, Madame."

This frightened her still more. Her heart was beating fast as she rapped on the door. Only the thought of the 18 francs sustained her courage.

"Come in!"

An impressive office! Three gentlemen were discussing something intently. Each of them, she observed, was decorated with the ribbon of the Legion of Honor.

"I—I have co-come here about an accident," she stammered.

"Please take a seat," one of the gentlemen said courteously. "I shall be at your service in a moment.

"And now, gentlemen. The company does not admit payment beyond 400,000 francs in this case. We cannot consider your claim for the other 100,000—out of the question. And the estimate, you must observe—"

"Very well. Court will decide the matter. There is nothing further for us to do but leave. Good day." The other two gentlemen bowed themselves out, very ceremoniously. There was absolutely no way for her to follow them.

"And now, Madame, how can I be of service?"

"I've come for this—" She held out the umbrella to his astonished gaze, fumbling awkwardly at the elastic. It was some time before she had it open. The gentleman looked at it pityingly.

"It is in a bad way, isn't it?" he said. "But what can I do for you?"

"It cost me 20 francs," she said. He was amazed.

"Really? So much? How expensive everything is these days! But if I may ask—what was it you wished to discuss with me?"

"But—it's *burnt*!"

The gentleman was not impressed.

"I am Mme. Oreille. We are insured here, and I've come to make a claim for this damage. But only to ask that you have it re-covered."

"But, madame—" the director said, "this is not an umbrella shop. We really can't make such repairs."

"No, but the price can be given to me, after I pay the bill and show it to you."

"But the claim is too trivial," he said patiently. "We couldn't possibly pay for every glove or handkerchief, broom or old slipper that was ever burnt."

"Well, sir, we had a fire last year that lost us 500 francs. M. Oreille made no claim then. In a small matter like this, you could surely—"

"You will admit, Madame, that M. Oreille has a strange procedure. He neglects a claim for 500 francs, and presses one of five or six francs.

"That's M. Oreille's affair," she answered. "The 500 francs was his loss. The 18 francs is mine. That's not the same thing at all."

By this time the director was weary of the business and inquired how the accident had happened. With the most thorough detail, the lady recounted how she had tried to light several matches for the candlestick on the shelf over her umbrella stand; how each in turn had failed. . . .

"Government matches, no doubt," remarked the director.

Mme. Oreille went on—how she retired, and smelled something smoldering. How she had always dreaded fire since the fire in the chimney, and nosed this one out like a bloodhound, sniffing here and there till she found the umbrella in its present condition, still smoking.

By this time the director begged her to fix a sum, her estimate of the damage.

"I will leave it to you to have it repaired. I have every confidence in you," she said in a burst of generosity. There was no telling how much she might get, she thought, if she did not state her figure too hastily.

"No, no, Madame. I cannot do that. Tell me what you want."

"Well . . . I think—I don't want to take advantage—suppose I just take this to a shop and cover it with good durable silk, and then bring the bill to you."

So it was arranged. The cashier gave her a card, ordering a refund on her repair bill. And she hurried out with the precious card, fearful lest the director change his mind. Now she walked along gaily, surveying critically the most fashionable shops of Paris—ah, yes, here was one, of a quite remarkable dignity and class. She walked in and up to the clerk without the least flicker of hesitation.

"This umbrella is to be covered with silk, really good silk. Use the very best you have. I am not particular about the price."

The Stolen White Elephant

Mark Twain

Samuel Langhorne Clemens (Mark Twain), American humorist (1835–1910)   A great favorite with many readers is Mark Twain; his jokes are still being repeated and his novels are read with pleasure.   He was a man of tremendous talent and inexhaustible humor. As a printer, miner, journalist, publisher, river pilot, essayist, novelist, secretary, and military officer, he acquired a wide experience.   He was very successful as a lecturer; and he wrote as he talked, for the ear more than for the eye. His best and most entertaining work is to be found when he is laughing at humbugs.

Great Britain once had a quarrel with the King of Siam over the matter of a boundary. The dispute was settled in favor of the British. The King of Siam, thought a handsome present to the British queen might restore confidence and good will. So he chose a white elephant, which only kings may possess, fit to reveal all his fine feelings and better intentions. And I, as a trusted British official then stationed in India, was given the task of taking the gift to London by way of the United States.

Well, we arrived safely in New York Harbor and we stabled the animal at Jersey City for a fortnight. But as luck would have it, the beast was stolen in the dead of night. A fearful calamity! I was just lucky enough to catch the chief of the New York detective force, Inspector Blunt, before he locked his office. That mastermind at once took up the matter and stood for a long time tapping his forehead and knitting his brows. There was no question—the man was thinking. That gave me great confidence in him. For several minutes after I had stated my case, in fact, he said nothing. Then he pledged me to secrecy.

"This is no ordinary case," he said. "I will see that the reporters only find out what it suits my ends to let them know. And now—to work! Name of the elephant?"

"Hassan Ben Ali Ben Selim Abdallah Mohammed Moise Alhammal Jamsetjcjeebhoy D'huleep Sultan Ebu Bhudpoor."

"Given name?"

"Jumbo."

"Place of birth? Parents? Brothers and sisters? Give a complete description, if you please, for every particular may be of the utmost importance."

This I did; and in the most efficient fashion the great man read back my description, to check. "Height, 19 feet; length from top of forehead to beginning of tail, 26 feet; total length, 48 feet. Footprints like print of a barrel upended in snow. Color, dull white; ear-piercings for jewelry, about the size of a plate; squirts water at total strangers; limps slightly; scar under left armpit; wore a castle containing seats for fifteen persons, when last seen."

When I had verified this, he handed it to his assistant, Alaric. "Fifty thousand copies at once! Send one to every detective office and pawnbroker on the continent. Send copies of this photograph, too. Too bad the trunk is curled up into the mouth—very misleading, as he does not usually hold it in that position. And now, about the reward. Let's see—suppose we offer a reward of $25,000 to begin with? Just a starter, you know. The thieves probably have friends everywhere who must be satisfied if we want to get back the elephant."

"Why bless my soul, do you know who they are?" I asked, already overawed by this gigantic intellect operating before me. The detective betrayed no emotion.

"Never mind that—I may and I may not. But mark my words, the man we are looking for is no pickpocket or mere hall thief. No beginner could have lifted your property, I'll tell you. They'll cover their traces carefully. Better start with at least 25,000." We started.

Inspector Blunt said that criminals have often been detected through peculiarities of appetite. The circular read as follows:

> Will eat anything from a man to a Bible, illustrated edition, bound in Russia leather, gold edges, 500 copies. Will drink half a ton of any liquid from Castor oil to carbolic acid—everything, that is, except European coffee—at a single time.

Well, the clear, decisive plans of the detective were nearly in full operation now.

"Captain Burns, tell Detectives Jones, Halsey, Bates, and Hackett to shadow the elephant. Send Detectives Moses, Dakin, Murphy, Rogers, Tupper, Higgins, and Bartholomew to shadow the thieves. Place a strong guard—30 men with 30 for relief—over the place where the elephant was stolen. They must keep strict watch and allow none to approach—except reporters—without written consent from me.

"Place detectives in plain clothes at all railway stations, steamship piers, and upon all roadways leading out of Jersey City to search all suspicious persons. Instruct them to search all trains and outgoing boats. Tap all telegraph offices. And let these things be done with the utmost secrecy—mind, the most impenetrable secrecy."

A moment the inspector sat in silence when his messengers had departed; then his blazing eyes were veiled.

"I am not given to boasting," he said. "It is not my habit.

But we shall find the elephant!" How warmly I thanked him, as confidence in his great powers increased within me!

As I had been ordered, I kept strict silence about the whole matter. But there must have been a leak somewhere, because next morning the papers were full of my misfortune. There were, in fact, 11 theories offered by various detectives, and 37 persons were named as suspects. It was revealed that the rear of the elephant's stable had been torn away; but this, as detectives explained carefully, was only a false clue planted by the criminals, who had managed the theft through some outlet as yet undiscovered. Chief Inspector Blunt himself put the blame for the theft squarely upon two known criminals, naming them publicly, in fact, as "Brick" Duffy and "Red" McFadden.

"We knew they were going to attempt this robbery ten days before they did it," he stated flatly, with a sagacity and foresight that amazed me.

"Why did you let them do it, if you knew they were going to?" I asked the great man. His answer was a lesson in method and understanding.

"It is not our job to prevent crime, but to punish it," he said. "We cannot punish a crime until it has been committed."

I remarked that our secrecy was ended by the newspapers. All of the facts, plans, and purposes of Blunt had been revealed. Even all suspected persons had been named and would now disguise themselves or go into hiding.

"Let them hide. I will find their secret places, as unerringly as the hands of fate. A detective must publish his theory, or else he will be supposed to have none."

Remarkable wisdom! I put down a considerable sum of money to meet expenses and read the newspapers carefully again. There I learned nothing further, except that the reward had been offered only to detectives if they caught the culprits. A moment later and the telegraph instrument was ticking. Darley had found tracks at Flower Station, New York; Baker had found a broken glass-factory at Barker's, N.J., and Hubbard had a clue too—a haystack on Long Island had disappeared during the night. Darley communicated again about the tracks. A farmer claimed they were holes he had dug to plant saplings. Inspector Blunt replied immediately.

"Arrest the man! Force him to name his pals! Continue to follow the tracks—to the Pacific if necessary."

Further news came from Ironville, N.Y. Hawes wrote that the elephant had thrown the village into a panic by killing a horse with a left-handed blow of the trunk. Hawes was saving a piece of the horse for evidence.

"Send 96 men to Ironville at once," said Inspector Blunt to Captain Burns. "Let them conduct their movements with the utmost secrecy."

Stumm wrote from Sage Corners, N.Y. The elephant had struck a lamppost and a policeman. Stumm had secured a portion of the policeman as a clue.

According to Brant, the elephant broke up a temperance meeting, and drowned several people by flooding them with water. O'Flaherty telegraphed from Hoganport: "Elephant raging in streets. Two plumbers passing; one killed. Other one escaped. Regret general."

The next telegram to arrive brought anger to the iron-willed Chief Inspector. "Barnum offers $4,000 a year for the privilege of posting circus posters on the elephant until your detectives find him," it read. For the first time I saw this masterly mind disturbed, a flush of anger on the granite countenance. In a moment he had dictated his answer to the insulting offer.

"Mr. Barnum's offer declined. Make it $7,000 or nothing." And in a few minutes, this great deal was completed.

Detective Mulrooney reported that the elephant dispersed a funeral at Bolivia, N.Y., and Detective Burke as well. Detective Brent reported that the poor elephant was plastered with circus posters from head to toe. Brent identified the elephant by description, except for the scar in the armpit. To make absolutely sure, Brown crawled under the elephant, and was crushed. The elephant escaped, wounded by cannon, and left a bloody trail all along his journey. That was the last telegraph report we received.

Newspapers next morning carried hardly anything besides this case. Inspector Blunt described it as "the greatest windfall any detective agency ever had." Besides reports of the numerous deaths and wrecks caused by the elephant's progress, there were the theories of 34 distinguished detectives published in full—and the theory of Detective Blunt printed in a separate column.

Two repeaters at the polls, a preacher and a lightning-rod salesman, had been stricken down during the night by what one reporter termed the "Scourge of Siam." Sixty persons in all had met death; and 240 had been wounded. Yet no trace of the thief could be found now. During the night, it seemed, he had found a perfect hiding place.

Citizens reported a swift glimpse of the vast bulk in Massachusetts, Pennsylvania, New Jersey, and even in downtown New York. But days passed without substantial clues. At Blunt's suggestion, my reward offer was raised to $75,000.

The newspapers, anxious for fresh sensations, were becoming sarcastic. But Inspector Blunt was calm and unaffected. We soon had to raise the offer to $100,000. Of this the faithful detectives, of course, would get half. I myself had long ago resigned myself to a life of poverty and disgrace with my government because of the misfortune; and the loss of my wealth now meant nothing.

Inspector Blunt immediately wrote an advertisement for the morning papers that read:

> A.—xwblv. 242 N. Tjnd—fz328wmlg. Ozpo—;
> 2 mo. ogw. Mum.

He said that if the thief was alive this would bring him to the usual meeting place.

When the reward was posted, we went to the great vaulted basements where our faithful detectives awaited further orders.

As I followed my great leader through a remote portion of the place, I saw him stumble on some massive object lying there, cloaked in darkness. "Our noble profession is justified," he cried as he fell. "Here is your elephant!"

Such a scene of rejoicing I have never known before. Feasting and champagne—the chief was the hero of the hour and his happiness was so complete and worthily won that it made me happy to see it, though I was a homeless beggar, and my priceless elephant was dead! In the midst of the excitement a telegram came from Darley in Michigan. He was following the tracks and would have the elephant in a week, he said.

"One of the finest minds on the force," Blunt said generously. And it was resolved to let him share in the reward.

Only one contemptible newspaper refused to praise Blunt as he deserved.

But poor Hassan was lost to me forever. The cannon shots had wounded him fatally and he had crept into this dangerous place in the fog, surrounded by enemies and in constant danger of detection till he died.

I am a ruined man and a wanderer on the earth. But my admiration for that man, whom I believe to be the greatest detective the world has ever produced, remains undimmed to this day.

The Celebrated Jumping Frog of Calaveras County

Mark Twain

It was in a mining camp out West that I first heard about Jim Smiley—strange character, if there ever was one. He would bet on anything, if he could only get someone to bet on the other side. Or, if he couldn't, why he'd simply switch sides; it made no difference to him what he was betting on.

He came out a winner almost every time, somehow. If there was a horse race, he'd have plenty of money afterwards; only once in a while he'd show up flat broke. Dog fight, cat fight, or chicken fight—he'd bet on it. Let two birds sit on a fence where someone saw them—he'd bet you which bird would fly off first. Or if a straddle bug started off for somewhere, Smiley would bet on how long it would take it to get there—wherever it was going! And if the straddle bug decided to make his trip go on to Mexico, there would be Jim Smiley taking the trip on to Mexico.

Folks around town said he would bet on anything and never even showed sense about what it was. There was a day once when Parson Walker's wife got sick, and everyone said she might never recover. Parson came into the saloon one morning, and Jim asked him politely how his wife was.

"Considerably better," says Parson. "Thank the Lord for His infinite mercy. With the blessing of Providence, she'll get well yet."

"Well," Jim blurts out before he even thought, "I'll bet two and a half dollars that she don't, anyway!"

Smiley had a mare that was the slowest thing you want to see. She had asthma too, and seemed about ready to pass away any time. But Jim would win on her nearly every race. They'd give her two or three hundred yards start, she looked so bad; and they'd pass her pretty soon. But near the end of the race, she'd get excited and desperate, and come galloping on, throwing her legs out in all directions, knocking fences to pieces, kicking up dust, raising a racket, coughing, sneezing, trumpeting through her nose—and she'd like as not fetch up at the judge's stand just a neck ahead.

His bull pup was named Andrew Jackson; not worth a cent to look at. Another dog could bully him, bite him, toss him away two or three times; Andrew Jackson acted as if he were perfectly satisfied. But when the bets were down, he'd grab the other dog by one joint of the hind leg; and he'd freeze on until the other dog had to give up—hour, or day, or a year if he had to. Smiley always won with that pup; until one day he matched him with a dog that didn't have any hind legs—had them caught in a circular saw, and they were sliced clean off. The money was all down, and Andrew Jackson made a snatch for the leg joint that just wasn't there. In a minute it was clear the poor dog didn't know what to do next and felt he'd been tricked. He gave Smiley one long look, as if to say his heart was broken and it was all *his* fault. Then he limped off a bit, and just lay down and died where he was.

One day Jim Smiley caught a frog. For three months hardly anyone ever saw him. He just sat in his back yard for the whole time and taught that frog how to jump. He'd give him just a little punch behind; the frog would go whirling up into the air like a doughnut, turn a somersault or two, and then come down flatfooted like a cat. This frog could catch a fly from as far off as he could see it. All he needed, Jim said, was an education; and Jim certainly made sure that he got it.

The frog would be set down on the floor, with plenty of

room on all sides; and Smiley would yell. "Flies, Daniel Webster! Flies!" Daniel Webster was the name he had given the frog. And the thing would spring right up and snag a fly off the counter and flop down again on the floor just like a gob of mud; and it would begin scratching the side of its head with its hind foot, as if it had no idea that it was a remarkable frog.

You never saw a frog so modest and straightforward as Daniel Webster. When it came to fair and square jumping at a dead level, he could get over more ground at one hop than any other animal of his breed. Jumping on a dead level was his strong point; on that, Jim Smiley would raise the bets up to his last cent. And he won quite a lot of money that way around the camp—mostly from strangers.

Smiley was so proud of this frog that he kept him in a little lattice box—used to bring it down to the bar, and wait around for a bet. And one day a stranger walked across the floor, getting more and more curious, and he asked Smiley,

"What might be you've got in that box?"

Jim looked around sort of idle and careless. "Might be a parrot," he said finally. "Or a canary, maybe. But it ain't. It's only just a frog."

The fellow took up the box, and turned it this way and that way, very carefully. "Hmm!" he said. "It's a frog all right. So it is. Well, what is *he* good for?"

"Good enough for one thing," Smiley drawled. "I reckon this frog can outjump any frog in Calaveras County."

The stranger studied the box long and patiently, and handed it back to its owner.

"Well," he said, "I don't see any p'ints about that frog that's any better than any other frog."

"Well, maybe you don't," Smiley answered. "Maybe you understand frogs, and maybe you don't understand them. Maybe you've had experience with these animals. Anyway, I have my opinion; and I'll just risk $40 that he can outjump any frog in Calaveras County."

The stranger studied the box a little longer, and then he

said in a sad, slow voice, "Now, I'm only a stranger here; and I ain't got any frog. But if I had a frog, I'd bet you." Smiley leaned forward all excited, and he said, "That's all right! That's all right! If you'll just hold my box a minute I'll go and get you a frog." And the man put down his $40 right next to Smiley's, and he picked up that box, and he just sat there waiting.

He sat there a good while, thinking and thinking to himself. Then he took the frog out of the box. He held him still, while he opened his mouth wide. And he took a teaspoon and filled that frog full of bird shot—filled him up pretty nearly to the chin and set him on the floor and waited.

Meanwhile Jim Smiley went to the swamp and slopped around in the mud for a long time. And at last he caught a frog and brought him in, holding him right carefully so the stranger could see he hadn't hurt him any. They set the new frog right down next to Daniel Webster, and Smiley said, without even a look at his frog, "Now if you're ready, stranger, I'll give the word."

The stranger nodded, and Smiley counted off, "One! Two! Three! Jump!" Then both of them touched off their frogs. The new one hopped off fine. But poor Daniel Webster gave a heave and stayed there. He hoisted up his shoulders with all his might, but he just stayed there. He wriggled this way and that, and his legs were scratching off in all directions, but it was no use. He just stayed there. He couldn't budge. He was planted solid as an anvil.

Smiley was surprised and disgusted, but he didn't have any idea what the trouble was.

The stranger took the money and started away, but when he was halfway out of the door he turned back again and jerked his thumb back over his shoulder at Daniel Webster. Very deliberately, he said again, "Well, *I* don't see any p'ints about that frog that's any better than any other frog."

Smiley stood scratching his head and looking down at the poor frog that lay there like a puddle of water. "I wonder if

there isn't something the matter with him. He appears to look mighty baggy, somehow." And he picked Daniel Webster up by the neck, and hefted him, and he said, "Why blame my cats if he doesn't weigh five pounds!"

So Jim turned the frog upside down and saw him belch out a double handful of shot. Then he saw how he had been tricked, and he was the angriest man you ever saw.

He set his frog down, and he lit out of the place like a train traveling over the prairie. But Jim Smiley never caught up with that stranger.

The Empty Drum

Count Leo Tolstoy

Count Leo Tolstoy, Russian Novelist (1828–1910)
Tolstoy was a Russian count who had more interest in
reforming society to help the underdog than he had in
enjoying the special privileges that were his. He spent a
good deal of his time educating poor peasants and his
great novels and stories show that he understood well
how much needs to be done for civilization. His novel
"War and Peace" and his short stories have great literary
skill as well as a passion for decent living.

Emilyan, the day laborer, walked through a meadow, and passing a frog, went out of his way to avoid harming it. "Emilyan," the day laborer heard, in a voice as sweet as honey. He turned and saw a lovely girl standing behind him.

"Why don't you marry, Emilyan?" she continued.

"How can I, my pretty maid? I have nothing in the world. Who would marry me?"

"Well, then, take me for your wife," she said. "All we'll have to do is to work hard and sleep less. We can find food and clothing in the city. Let us live there."

The girl was very attractive to Emilyan. "Very well," he answered. "Let's be married."

At the outskirts of the city they set up housekeeping in

a little cottage where they were very happy. But one day the king passed their cottage and saw the wife of Emilyan. He stopped his carriage.

"How could you who are such a beautiful woman marry a peasant?" he asked.

"Thank you," she replied. "But I am well content with my husband."

When the king rode on he kept thinking of her, however, trying to find a way to get her to be his queen at the palace. Then he summoned his counselors for suggestions.

"Get Emilyan to work here," they told him. "We'll see that he is worked to death, and the lady will become a widow." And so it was planned.

When Emilyan was told that he must work at the king's palace, he was disturbed somehow; and that evening he talked it over with his wife.

"Go to the palace and work there during the day," she told him. "Do just as the king tells you. But I shall remain home; and, every evening, you return to this cottage. And all will be well."

The next morning Emilyan came alone to his new work, and the king's steward gave him enough to do to tire out two strong men. Without hope of succeeding, Emilyan began, and when evening came it was finished. He was given four men's work for the next day. He returned to his cottage to find everything ready for him and his wife to welcome him.

"Don't be frightened of your work," she told him at supper. "Keep right on working, looking neither behind to what is done, nor ahead to what must be done. Then all will be well." So Emilyan slept, and worked next day without turning. By twilight he was finished and turned his steps homeward.

And each day his tasks were increased. But when night came, lo, they were finished while he worked looking neither before nor behind him. Then the king's servants saw they could not harm him with rough work, and gave him skilled tasks to perform—carpentry, masonry, and roofing—but each night saw his tasks fairly accomplished.

In two weeks the king had grown very angry at his counselors and accused them of mocking him. "This man goes to his work hale and hearty every day," he said.

"The man or his wife must know magic," they answered. "But we can still trap him. If you will send for him and command him to build a cathedral in a single day, we can make him pay the penalty of death for his failure."

So it was arranged. In the evening the king summoned Emilyan and ordered him to build a cathedral by the next evening in the square opposite his palace. "If it is ready on time I shall reward you," said the king. "But failure on your part will make us take your head off."

Emilyan grew pale. This time he was really frightened. "Well, the end is at hand now. I can never meet such conditions," he thought, and departed sadly homeward.

"Get everything ready, wife," he said. "We must escape from the king or I am lost."

"Why should we run away?" she asked. And he told her of his latest task.

But his wife would not hear of flight. "The king has too many soldiers," she said. "Wherever we go they will find us. There is no escaping him. As long as we have strength, we must try to obey him. For the present, little father, only eat your supper and go to bed. Then get up a little earlier tomorrow morning, and everything will be well."

And the peasant slept through the night, till his wife awakened him on the next morning. "Here are nails and a hammer. Go and build your cathedral; that will be enough work for the day."

When he came to the square, there was a great cathedral almost finished. He set at once to work upon it, and sure enough it was finished by evening. When the king awoke next morning, he looked out to find Emilyan driving the last nails. He was angered beyond measure that he still could

not marry the wife of the peasant; and he summoned his counselors.

"You must find a better plan than those you have tried so far," he said. "Or else I shall treat you as we have tried to treat the peasant."

"Let the peasant construct a river about the palace and have ships sailing upon it," they proposed.

And this too was ordered. "If you can build a cathedral in a day, this should be easy," the king told Emilyan. "Only see that it is ready tomorrow, else I shall have your head for it."

Once more Emilyan returned disheartened, thinking only of escape. Once more his wife persuaded him simply to sleep, and awake early in the morning. "Go to the city," she said when she had awakened him. "There at the wharf you will find only one mound left to finish. Take your spade and level it."

And sure enough, when he came to the city the simple peasant beheld a great river, glittering and splendid, encircling the city. And behold, ships were sailing upon its waters, and some lay quietly at anchor. And the king, amazed and angry, saw Emilyan leveling the last mound just outside his window.

This time the king's counselors were frightened and came forth themselves with a new suggestion to dispose of Emilyan. "You must send him on an errand," they told the king. "Bid him go you know not whither, and fetch you know not what. Then, whatever he brings, wherever he goes, he will be wrong. You can behead him then for his fault."

For the first time the king was pleased, and sent Emilyan upon his errand: to go, he knew not whither; and fetch, he knew not what. When the wife heard this she did not take it quite so calmly, but thought the matter over with great care.

"You will have to go to my old grandmother, the peasant woman, for help in this matter," she said finally. "They are learning to trap us. My grandmother will give you something to take to the palace. Take it; and when you get there, you will find me waiting for you. This time they are going to get me to the palace by force. But do not be afraid; only obey my grandmother, and all will be well. Now take this wallet and the spindle. Give them to my grandmother and she will know you are my husband."

Beyond the city went Emilyan, where he saw a company of soldiers drilling. When they sat down to rest he drew up to them. "My brothers," he said, "can you direct me to go I know not whither and fetch I know not what? I must go upon this errand for the king."

The soldiers were amazed. "We could never help you

brother," they said. "From the day we became soldiers we have been going, we know not whither, and fetching we know not what."

As Emilyan went on, he found a little hut in the forest where an old peasant woman was spinning flax and weeping. To her Emilyan gave the spindle and told her the whole story of his marriage, and tasks, and his errand. At this, she ceased her weeping. "Sit down and eat," she said.

When he was finished, she gave him a ball of yarn. "Unroll it before you until you come to the last house in a great city. There you must take lodging. You will see something that men obey sooner than father and mother. And this you must take to the king.

"If the king refuses it, say, 'If it is not the right thing it must be beaten and broken.' Then take it to the river, smash it and pitch it into the water; and you will recover your wife."

Now, the unrolling ball of yarn took Emilyan to the seashore, where he found the city and took his lodging in a great house.

Early in the morning, he heard a father order his son to cut firewood; but the boy refused. "But your father's bones ache!" cried the mother. "Will you let *him* do it?" And still the boy dozed on.

But suddenly there were crashing noises in the street. The boy leapt up to dress and followed the sounds. And Emilyan looked to see what it was he had obeyed, sooner than his father or mother.

A man walked through the streets and pounded a round thing with two sticks as he walked. It was like a tub with skins stretched over the ends. "It is called a drum," someone told Emilyan. All that day Emilyan followed the drummer until he lay down to sleep. Then Emilyan snatched up the drum and ran off with it to his own city.

Sure enough, his wife was not at his cottage; so he went straight to the palace. They had taken her to the king.

"Tell the king," said Emilyan, "that I have gone, I know

not whither, and fetched I know not what." And at this the king came forth.

"Where have you been?" he asked.

"I do not know," answered Emilyan.

"And what have you brought?"

Emilyan held the drum up to him. But the king turned away, refusing to see it. "That is not it," said the king.

"Well, if it is not the right thing, it must be beaten," said Emilyan. He began beating the drum and marched out of the palace. As he did so, the king's army followed him, saluting the peasant and asking his commands. The king shouted to his army, to prevent them from following Emilyan; but they would heed nothing except the drum.

When the king saw this, he gave orders that the wife of Emilyan be returned to the peasant and asked Emilyan for the drum.

"No," Emilyan answered. "I must beat this thing, and break it, and pitch the scraps into the river." And he walked to the river, carrying the drum, followed by the soldiers. There at the bank he beat the drum into pieces and cast the pieces into the waters. At once the soldiers ran off in all directions. And Emilyan took his wife and brought her home. The king ceased to trouble them, and they lived happily forever after.

The System of Dr. Tarr and Prof. Fether

Edgar Allan Poe

Edgar Allan Poe, American poet and story writer (1809–1849) Poe's mind seems to have been stocked with the most wonderful terrors. From the weird music of The Raven *to his famous horror stories—yes, even in his humorous yarns—there is a grim undercurrent. Born Edgar Poe in Boston, he was adopted by Mr. and Mrs. John Allan in Richmond. As a result of misunderstandings with Mr. Allan, Poe left college and home and enlisted in the army as a private. Later Mr. Allan bought him out of the army and procured a commission for him at West Point from which he was expelled. Known as the creator of the modern detective story, Poe was a critic, poet, and writer of fascinating tales.*

One day as I was on a tour in the south of France, I chanced to meet a gentleman who knew M. Maillard, then head of a private mental hospital located nearby. I was rather interested in the subject of mental illness at that time. I had heard wonderful reports of Dr. Maillard's famous soothing system. And so I resolved, if my new friend would introduce me, to visit the asylum.

To this my friend objected. He was in a hurry, he said. He wanted to get on with his journey. And he had the usual and common horrors about lunatics. He would consent only to introduce me to M. Maillard and continue on his way without entering the place. That was good enough for me.

The asylum proved to be a fantastic building, quite neglected and desolate. For a moment, I shared my friend's feelings. But M. Maillard very soon reassured me. A conservative gentleman of great dignity, he led me at once to his drawing room, which was furnished with excellent taste, and rich with books, drawings, and musical instruments.

Seated at a piano there was a young and beautiful lady singing. She was dressed in mourning and showed a becoming dignity both when she sang and when she acknowledged our introduction most charmingly.

According to reports, M. Maillard's "soothing system" allowed his patients all possible liberty around the asylum, observing them secretly only when necessary. Hence there was some doubt in my mind about the lady before me. Her eyes were unnaturally bright, though her words and manner were restrained and intelligent. Perhaps—

I spoke very guardedly on the most general topics and received very sensible replies. Still, there were so many cases, apparently quite sane. As soon as the young lady had left the room, I shot an inquiring glance at my host. "No!" he said instantly. "Oh, no indeed. My niece. A member of the family, and a most accomplished young woman." And as graciously as possible, he put aside my apologies for my awkward suspicion of her sanity.

"When my former system was in operation," he said, "the patients could be seen all about. But we have stopped that practice, because of the great dangers it caused."

I expressed some surprise. I had never heard that his system had been changed. I still considered him, in fact, the outstanding advocate of the "soothing system." Would he please, then, explain his methods?

"Well, we were accustomed to curing our patients by humoring them," M. Maillard said quietly. "Some men, for example, fancied they were chickens. We treated that as fact. We ridiculed them when they did anything *unlike* a chicken, fed them only a little corn and gravel—that worked wonders.

"Another device was to set each to guard the actions of the others. By giving them confidence, we gained their confidence and saved the expense of a number of keepers as well. Never any punishments; the violent cases we quickly removed to public hospitals, of course.

"But all that is of the past now. My new method is much better—the best, I believe. But I don't wish to spoil your appetite for dinner. We shall dine first, and when your nerves are steadier, inspect the place."

At six o'clock the dining room was filled with about thirty people, all rather wildly attired, without the best of taste, I fear. Women over seventy showed a blaze of jewelry, bracelets, earrings—poorly made dresses—well, there was M. Maillard's niece, anyhow! But dressed how curiously! An enormous hooped skirt, soiled cap of Brussels lace, much too large for her. For a while I thought M. Maillard had deceived me, that I was dining with his patients, unannounced.

Then I remembered. They were southern French provincials, of course, odd and old-fashioned in their notions.

Three walls of the room were heavily windowed and every window was barred and shuttered. Wax tapers lighted everything in a blinding glare. Food and drink were all about on tremendous platters. I resolved to enjoy without wonder, like a wise traveler.

The company was well educated and spoke with the greatest freedom—even pleasure, I should say—about lunacy.

A fat little gentleman piped up: "We had a fellow here once thought he was a teapot. Amazing, how many people think they are teapots! This one polished himself every morning with buckskin!" A tall man opposite broke in. "How about the one who thought he was a donkey? Ate nothing but thistles and always kicked up his heels, like this. . . ."

"Keep your feet to yourself, sir," an old lady near him cried. "You needn't illustrate quite so practically! You're only acting naturally, I believe!" The gentleman had begun to apologize by drinking a toast to the lady. But just then three strong waiters appeared carrying a great platter. On it was a small calf, roasted whole, on its knees, with an apple in its mouth.

My host pressed it upon me, but I insisted that I preferred the rabbit.

"Pierre!" cried my host. "Give this gentleman a piece of our *rabbit-au-chat*!"

"Thank you," I said hastily, "No thank you! On second thought, never mind the cat-of-rabbit, or rabbit-of-cat. I'll just have this ham here!"

"There was a patient who thought he was a cheese," shouted a man at the foot of the table. But another cut in.

"He was a fool—simply a fool! Now the man who was a bottle of champagne—*he* went off—pop!—every so often, and he fizzed—fizzzed—fizzzzed."

M. Maillard looked very severely at the speaker. A little fellow in a big wig took over.

"I wish you could have seen our man who thought himself a frog! Croaked incessantly—gluggg! gluggg!—rolled up his eyes, distended his mouth—really, you'd just have to admire his genius!"

"Or what about Jules Desoulières, who was sure he was a pumpkin? Wanted the cook to make him into a pie, which he'd never do. But really, I'm not sure this pie a là Desoulières wouldn't be a very fine dish indeed—a very fine dish!"

"Well, yes, of course," I said, looking fixedly at M. Maillard. He laughed unreservedly.

"Droll fellow! Quite a wit! You must understand him," he said to me calmly.

"Or—or Boulard, the pinwheel! Could spin on one heel for an hour, like this—" The illustration was remarkable, but I was distracted from it by an old lady, who called out loudly:

"Pinwheel? an absurd notion! But there's some sense to Mme. Joyeuse. She learned that by some accident she had become a rooster. So she behaved very sensibly! Flapped her wings and crowed quite deliciously—Ur-er-er Ur-Ur!"

"Madame Joyeuse! Behave yourself!" cried our host angrily; and the old lady blushed and hung her head.

The young lady I had first met now modestly related her story of Eugenie Salsafette, who wanted to dress by getting *outside* her clothes, not *inside.* She certainly would have shown us the process, over the horrified protests of the company; but we were all startled by loud yells and shrieks from the main hall. My nerves were certainly affected, but I never saw such terror as my companions exhibited. Shrinking and pale, they shivered and chattered with terror, listening as the sounds came nearer. But the cries ceased and the company grew calm instantly.

I took the opportunity to question M. Maillard about our fellow guests. "They are quite harmless?" I asked.

"Harmless!" he cried. "Why, what do you mean? They are my friends and my keepers! Best lunatic nurses in the world. The women too—their bright eyes are very effective— fascinate the patients, like snakes. You mustn't mind their ways. We're not stuffy here, you know, in the south! Do pretty much as we please—and the wine, you know—rather heady stuff!"

"And your new system?" I continued. "Is it your own invention?" I had to shout a little, over the noise of the table.

"Well, not entirely," he replied modestly. "Some portions were invented by Doctor Tarr, of course you've heard of him! And I've gotten a good deal from the work of the celebrated Fether —Professor Fether! You know his works, of course?"

With the utmost confusion, I had to confess ignorance. I was really ashamed of myself.

But my host carried it off generously by offering me a glass of wine. The company meanwhile had made liberal use of the bottles and were engaged in all sorts of weird and noisy enterprises that made conversation difficult. In addition, a band of musicians had established themselves and were playing what they must have fondly imagined was music. To my mind, it simply made the din perfectly impossible.

My host used the time to enlighten me about the defects of his old "soothing system" and its dangers. Every word increased in volume with the noise of the room until we were shrieking our remarks at each other.

"The more sensible a lunatic appears, the more dangerous he or she is," M. Maillard shouted. "And those wandering about the institution were very cunning schemers indeed. In fact," he informed me, "quite recently—*very* recently, in fact, the inmates successfully plotted to overthrow their keepers. Bound the keepers hand and foot, imprisoned them, and then ran the institution to suit themselves, under the leadership of a foolish fellow who imagined he had invented a new system of government."

"But of course, the situation was soon remedied," I yelled to him. "Visitors coming in, the cries of the keepers, the people of the countryside—they would give the alarm?"

"There you are quite wrong," shrieked my host. "The inmates were too cunning for that. Never let in any visitors, except one very stupid young man, who could be led by the nose as long as necessary. And the lunatics had a fine time.

Made free with the family wardrobe and jewels. Raided the cellars, which were well stocked with wine—lived well, I can tell you. And started a very simple, neat system to control their keepers."

Here louder cries from outside cut him short. There was no doubt that the room was being invaded.

"The lunatics are loose!" I cried. M. Maillard, quite shamelessly, I thought, threw himself under the sideboard. The musicians leaped up, and playing for the first time in unison, broke into "Yankee Doodle." The pinwheel whirled, the champagne bottle popped, the frog croaked, the donkey brayed, the rooster crowed.

The great shutters of the room were breaking under a steady attack from outside. They crashed in together, and a troop of strange creatures like apes rushed in upon us. I received a terrible beating and rolled under the table unconscious. When I awoke, I was imprisoned and remained so for a month.

And in that time, I succeeded in solving the whole puzzle to my satisfaction. You see, M. Maillard had once been head of the institution. But his own head having given way some years before, he had become an ordinary patient. With the help of his fellow patients, just as he had described the thing to me at dinner, he had overpowered the keepers, tarred and feathered them, and put them carefully away in the cells, keeping them on a generous diet of bread and water. The latter was pumped over them daily.

But one keeper finally escaped by a sewer and released the rest. The "soothing system," I am happy to say, was finally restored at the institution. But I can't help thinking that M. Maillard was right about his method. It was simple, neat, and gave no trouble.

Yet, although I have searched every library in Europe, I cannot seem to find the works of Dr. Tarr, nor those of the famous Professor Fether.

The Sphinx

Edgar Allan Poe

Cholera was terrifying New York, but by good fortune I was able to escape to the home of my cousin, who invited me to spend a fortnight with him in his home on the banks of the Hudson.

What an ideal summer vacation that might have been, were it not for the dreadful shadow that hovered over it! The woods there were excellent for our summer rambles, and well worth sketching. There was boating and fishing and swimming. At home, there were fine books, and music—everything to make our hours pass pleasantly—but dark messages came again and again from the stifling city to the southward.

The approach of a messenger was horrible to us, for almost every day it heralded the death of some friend or acquaintance. For my part, the very air that blew from the south seemed to be hot with death, laden with disease and foulness. My host had a healthier mind. The real misfortunes affected him deeply enough; but the fancied ones that tortured my feverish mind had no power to move him.

His own spirits were low, I realize now, but at any time he could find enough cheerfulness to strengthen me with his remarkable comments, sound reasoning, and words of solid good sense.

He would make it a point to talk with me about anything

general, about anything that could not cause worry. A good deal of our time, on our rambles and at home, was spent in conversation, where I noticed the force and understanding in his remarks.

One of his favorite points was this: that human error very often crept into our thinking through a failure of *proportion,* or *perspective*; an element of distance, or of time, might cause an error of which we are not aware. Suppose, for example, we discussed the important question of democracy and its effect on mankind. Before we could judge that effect, we must reckon how long it would take for democracy to become generally accepted—how quick a rate may be expected—for our results will be altered by that rate of progress.

"Can you name a single writer on the subject of government who has even discussed that question? To them, the subject doesn't even seem worthy of discussion. . . ."

I am afraid that some of his efforts to rouse me out of my fears and fancies were useless. His library was crowded with volumes of mystic books which could be expected to arouse the imagination and feed it with superstitious fancies. These books I read secretly, against his excellent advice.

One of my favorite beliefs was in omens and warnings. At that time I really believed that they predicted natural events.

"Why, that's ridiculous!" my cousin insisted. "For every bit of evidence you present for an omen, I can show a dozen for simple chance, a thousand cases of omens that foretold nothing and were promptly forgotten. Naturally, if you keep on looking for omens, you will have half a dozen collected for yourself whenever there happens to be a catastrophe. But have you ever kept track of the omens that were wasted?"

"Well," I insisted doggedly, "this idea of natural warnings has been with people since the beginning of time. It begins in all places and countries, among all peoples. To say that it grows up by chance in so many different places, spontaneously, and yet has no foundation, is very hard to believe."

That very evening something happened that utterly confounded me and fixed my notion and fear of omens more firmly than ever. The day had been hot, and I sat book in hand by the open window, gazing down a long view of the river and a distant hill beyond. The face of that hill had been shaved by a.landslide, as I saw. Only a few enormous trees were left standing. This I noticed mechanically, while my thoughts wandered to the stricken city below. My eyes rose a second time to the hill and remained there, fixed by amazement. From the summit of the bare hill, a living and hideous monster was making its swift way down to the bottom, where it disappeared into the deeper foliage. Either my mind or my eyes must have deceived me, it seemed. I spent some time convincing myself that I was in my senses.

By a comparison of the monster with the few remaining trees that it passed in its progress—enormous trees they were, to have withstood the slide—I saw that it was much larger than an ordinary battleship. In fact, in general outline it faintly resembled one. The beast had a mouth situated at the end of a trunk that stretched some 60 or 70 feet—it was as thick as the whole body of an elephant.

The root of the trunk lay in black shaggy hair—more than the coats of 20 buffalos could have provided; and two gleaming tusks swept downward from the mass. On each side of the long trunk, some 30 or 40 feet in length, I judged, a gigantic staff extended, made evidently of pure crystal, shaped in the form of a prism; the rays of the setting sun were reflected gorgeously through these prisms in the distance. Also extending from the trunk of this incredible animal, there were two pairs of wings outspread, each nearly a hundred yards in length, one pair above the other, and every wing covered with immense metal scales, ten or twelve feet in diameter. The upper and lower wings were connected by a strong chain.

But the most startling thing of all was the breast of this animal. A death's head covered its entire surface, traced in glaring white upon a black background, as if some accurate artist had drawn it there.

This terrific animal I saw with horror and awe. Something fearful was foretold by it, I knew, and there was nothing my reason could tell me to deny this. The thing was there. I saw it. I was awake and sensible, yet I saw it.

Even as I watched, the great jaws at the end of the trunk swung open. Just as the monster was disappearing at the base of the hill, a sound of woe, a cry that struck my ears like a death knell, reached me, and I fell to the floor unconscious. I cannot tell what feeling of dread, what self-distrust, prevented me from telling my cousin of the experience, but for three or four days I withheld it.

One evening we sat together in that self-same room, I at the window, he lounging nearby. With my eyes on the hill,

I gave him a full account of the experience, to which he listened impatiently, interrupting with laughter which grew less and less natural as I proceeded. It was clear that he thought I was going insane. But just at this instant I looked to the hill, and—there was the monster! My shout of terror brought my host to look fixedly where I pointed. I traced its progress for him, minutely. No. He could see nothing.

By this time I was really frightened, I can tell you. If the thing was not a sign of death, it was at least a pretty sure sign of madness. Passionately, I fell back in my chair, to cover my face with my hands. When I looked again, the creature had disappeared.

My host seemed to have struck a thought, however; for he now began to question me more closely on the appearance of the animal, which I described very faithfully. Wherever I could, I played down the unbelievable features. Yet I confess the description seemed, even in my own ears, like a bad dream. Nothing like that could ever have walked down that hillside. None but a disordered mind could have seen it.

Yet my cousin seemed by degrees to grow relieved. After a time he sighed deeply, as though he had cast off a great burden, and with the most maddening calmness started a long general discussion. It was the last subject which we had mentioned, the failure of people to think of their problems with a true sense of proportion.

"We are constantly underrating or exaggerating our object," he droned on, as I only half listened. "Because we will never make the right allowance for its nearness or distance."

Here he paused to search in the book case, while I watched him sadly, wondering what the end must be for me in this matter which he took so lightly. He picked out a book on natural history and asked me to exchange places with him. The fine print, he said, could be made out only near the better light of my window. I complied dully, watched him sit there in silence for a moment, and then heard him in the same calm voice continue his discourse.

"You know, if it were not for the sharp details you observed and the accurate description you gave me of this awful monster, I could never have told you anything about it. But here is an account that may interest you, a schoolbook description of the genus *sphinx,* of the family *crepuscularia,* order of *lepidoptera,* class of *insecta*—or, in other words, an insect.

"'Four membranous wings covered with tiny metallic scales; mouth making a rolling trunk formed by the long jaws, near which are lower jaws and downy feelers; lower wings fixed to the upper by a stiff hair; antennae, prismatic and club-shaped. The Death's Head Sphinx causes terror by a melancholy cry which it utters and the sign of death that appears upon its body.'"

Here my lecturer looked up at my open mouth and staring eyes and closed the book gently to lean forward into the exact position I had taken when I saw the monster. There he remained for a time.

"Yes. Here it is now," he said finally. "A remarkable creature it is, to be sure. It's going up that hill again, I see. But, do you know?—I think it's not nearly so large as you think—nor quite so far away for that matter. The fact is— the fact is, it seems to be wriggling right now up this spider thread along the window sash. Yes. . . .

"The creature is about a sixteenth of an inch long at most. As I am watching it now, it must be about that same distance—about a sixteenth of an inch—away from the pupil of my eye. And there, my imaginative friend—there is your terrible monster!"

Three Sundays in a Week

Edgar Allan Poe

For my whole life I have lived with my Uncle Rumgudgeon. My parents, when they died, left me to him in their will.

A fine old English gentleman he was, too, but with a few weak points. He was proud, passionate, pompous, with a red nose, thick skull, and a fat bank account. He had a full sense of his own importance. He was positive and cranky. If you asked him for anything, his first answer was always "No!"

But he was not ill-willed, as people imagined. In the long run, there were few requests which he would not finally grant. The longer he resisted, the more generous he was likely to be. Even an attack on his purse, strongly as he opposed it, would generally bring a handsome present.

He thought of himself as a kind of scientist, not because he had troubled to study science, but once someone had mistaken him for the celebrated Doctor Double L. Dee, the quack lecturer on physics. Ever since then, the doctor, Double L. Dee, became his oracle. Science was everything, he said. Poetry was a silly waste of time, he said. The stuff I was writing was trash, he said; and it gave him something to laugh at—loudly and often. Well, the old villain probably meant nothing by it—liked me well enough—nearly as well as he liked his own daughter, Kate, with whom I was brought up.

But it was a dog's life he led me. From my first to my fifth years, he used to give me regular beatings. From five to fifteen years, he threatened me with Reform School. From fifteen to twenty years, not a day passed without his promise to cut me off without a penny.

Kate was a good friend, though. She told me very sweetly that we could be married any time I might talk my old Uncle Rumgudgeon into giving his consent. Without that, we couldn't touch her money until she was 21—and that was a good many years to wait without any money of my own.

In vain we begged his mercy. There was nothing in the world he wanted more than our marriage. But, since we had been rash enough to ask him, why that was the end of it. He must refuse. I think he would have given ten thousand dollars from his own pocket (Kate's money was her own) to get some strange excuse for consenting. But there it was. His refusal was already on the record!

One afternoon the old bear was sitting with his feet on the mantelpiece and a cup of wine in his paw.

"My *dear* Uncle," I said, "you are always *so* very considerate, and have shown your kindness in *so* many ways, that—well, that I feel I have only to make one suggestion, to be sure of your—well, your good will, as it were. . . ."

"Hem. Good boy! Go on," he said.

"I am sure, my very dear uncle (you rascal!) that you really have no *serious* intention of stopping my marriage with Kate . . . just a joke of yours. I know—ha, ha—how very *pleasant* you are at times!"

"Ha, ha, ha! Blast you, yes!" said my uncle.

"To be sure—I knew you were joking all along. Now, Uncle, all that Kate and I ask is that you help us with a little advice—that is, regarding the date, you know—in short, when would it be most convenient for yourself, that the wedding shall—shall come off, you know?"

"Come off? Come off, you scoundrel? What do you mean by that? Better wait till it goes on, I say!"

"Haa—haa-hee—hee—huu-hu—that's fine! That's very good indeed! Goes on, not comes off—that's capital. But really now, what we'd like to know is this. What is the time that you would indicate for it *precisely*, you know?

"Wouldn't it be enough, Bobby, if I just left it at random—some time within a year or so, for example? Must it be *precisely*?"

"Why—well, if you please, Uncle—"

"Say no more, Bobby my boy, say no more. You're a fine fellow, you are, and we'll make it *precisely*. Since you will have the exact time, why, we'll oblige you for once. You shall have my consent—and her inheritance. We mustn't forget the inheritance—let me see—when shall we make it? Today's Sunday, isn't it? Well, then, you shall be married *precisely*—precisely, mind you,—when three Sundays come together in a week. Do you hear me, sir? Stop gaping at nothing, you young villain. I say you can have Kate and her money when three Sundays come together in a week— but not *till* then. Not till then, if I die for it. You know me. I'm a man of my word. Now be off!" And with that he raised his glass of wine and began gulping it as I rushed out of the room.

This was trouble indeed! I cursed myself for not having let well enough alone. For, if there was one thing I knew for certain, it was that I should never have Kate and his consent until he could actually say in truth that three Sundays had fallen upon the same week. There was no question of it.

Now it so happened that among Kate's sailor friends were two men who had just traveled around the globe. They had circled it in a year and come back to England. With their help, Kate and I tried to gain our point indirectly. So we invited the pair up to meet my uncle, and after a half hour or so of idle talk, we began to steer the conversation.

"Well, well, Mr. Rumgudgeon," Captain Pratt started. "Here I am just a year after leaving England—let me see, October 10—yes, just a year since I called here, you will remember, to bid my friends goodbye. By the way—it *does* seem a coincidence, really, doesn't it? Captain Smitherton here has also been absent a year exactly—just a year today!"

"Why yes, yes, yes," replied my uncle. "Very queer indeed. Both of you gone just a year—very queer indeed. Now, that's what Dr. Double L. Dee would call an extraordinary concurrence of events. Extraordinary! Doctor Doub—"

"To be sure, papa, it *is* something strange," Kate interrupted hastily. "But remember that Captain Pratt didn't go by the same route as Captain Smitherton—that makes a difference, you know."

"Well," broke in my uncle. "I don't know any such thing! How should I? It only makes the thing even more extraordinary."

"Why papa, Captain Pratt went around Cape Horn, and Captain Smitherton doubled the Cape of Good Hope."

"Precisely—the one went east and the other went west, you fool! And they both have gone completely around the world. Now, Dr. Double L. Dee—"

"Captain Pratt, you must come and spend the evening with us tomorrow," I said, "—you and Captain Smitherton. You can tell us all about your voyages, and we'll have a game of cards—"

"Cards? My dear fellow, you forget!" cried Captain Pratt. "Tomorrow will be Sunday, you know. Some other evening!"

"Sunday?" Kate demanded. "Come, you know Robert's not so bad as that! *Today* is Sunday, of course!"

"To be sure! To be sure!" my uncle added.

"I must beg both your pardons," Pratt insisted, "but I can't be so much mistaken. I know tomorrow's Sunday, because—"

Here Smitherton found his voice at last. He'd been looking at the others as though they were mad. "What *are* you people thinking about, anyhow? Wasn't *yesterday* Sunday, I should like to know?"

Everyone had an answer for that, but they were different

answers. "Today's Sunday!" my uncle roared, purple with anger. "No! No! Tomorrow's Sunday," called Pratt.

"Why, you are all mad, every one of you! I am as positive that yesterday was Sunday as I am that I'm sitting in this chair."

And here Kate ended the quarrel by jumping up, as if she had a new thought. "I see it all! I see it all! It's a judgment on you, papa, about you know what! It's a very simple thing, really. I can explain it in a minute. Here's Captain Smitherton—he says yesterday was Sunday. And so it was. He's right. Bobby and Uncle and I say *today* is Sunday. And we're right. We're perfectly right. And Captain Pratt is right too, when he says *tomorrow* is Sunday.—We're all right, because *three Sundays have come together in this week!*"

"Why, of course! said Smitherton after a bit of mock thought. "What fools we two are!"

"The earth you know, is about 24,000 miles around. And

it spins around from west to east in 24 hours. Now if I sail along eastward a thousand miles from this position, I reach London with an hour extra, because I've been traveling right towards the rising sun and meeting it as it rose. In that way, I gain an hour on the clock. I see the sun rise just an hour before you do. And in another thousand miles eastward, I gain another hour in the same way—by meeting the sun before it rises. Thus when I go eastward around the globe, 24,000 miles or so, and reach this spot again, why, I've gone toward the rising sun just 24 hours. That is to say, when I arrive, it is a full day ahead of your time. Understand?"

"But Dr. Double L. Dee—" my uncle began feebly. Smitherton would not be interrupted.

"But Captain Pratt, on the contrary, traveled westward. Every thousand miles took him an hour away from the rising sun. Each thousand miles in *that* direction brought him to a point an hour further from the sun. It takes just an hour for the sun to catch up with him there. So we can say that he has lost an hour. When he has sailed 24,000 miles west, why, he has lost just 24 hours. He has arrived a day *after* our time.

"Now, in that way, yesterday was really Sunday for me, because I gained a day. With you, Mr. Rumgudgeon, who remained here, today is Sunday. Captain Pratt, however, lost a day. Tomorrow will be his Sunday.

"And what is even more interesting, Mr. Rumgudgeon, there can be no particular reason given why the day of any one of us should be more correct than another. We are all perfectly correct in our claims about this Sunday."

"My eyes! yes! yes! yes!" said my uncle, thoroughly confused. "This is a judgment! But I'm a man of my word— you shall have her, Bobby, inheritance and all, when you please. I'm a man of my word, I say! Three Sundays in a *week,* all in a row! *Three* Sundays in a week! Three *Sundays* in a week! By Jove, I'll go and tell Dr. Double L. Dee about that one, I can tell you!"

Con Cregan's Legacy
Charles Lever

*Charles Lever, Irish writer (1806–1872) Charles Lever
was a journalist, doctor, and novelist. This Irishman was
known in his own time as a brilliant and amazing novelist, writing some thirty-seven volumes. He loved a joke
and played up farce in his writing. There is very little
subtlety and suggestion, but a great deal of laughter and
unexpected turns of plot in his work.*

Con Cregan was my father, and a shrewd man he was. His
cabin stood right at the borders of two counties, Meath and
King's. And since the two counties were always arguing which
of them had his land, he would pay taxes to neither until they
settled it. But when it came to voting, why there he was at
the elections, first in the balloting in Meath, and then in
King's.

Would you like to know how my father got the land
called "Con's Acre"? It's a fine story that shows all my
father's shrewdness.

The richest man in our parish was a farmer, Harry McCabe.
He had two mean, ill-tempered sons, Peter, the elder, and Mat,
the younger. They would fight and squabble all day, until at
last Mat got tired of it. He set off for the city of Dublin, enlisted in the army and was sent off to India. The old farmer

grieved about it and grew sick, while Peter, the elder brother, kept telling him he should leave none of his property to Mat. He should make a will, he said, and leave everything to Peter.

Old Harry McCabe said "Never!" His two sons would get equal shares when he was gone, and that was that. Far into the night we could hear them quarrelling when we passed the place: first the old man's voice, weak and reedy, then Peter's deep, hoarse voice, and then both together for a while. One Sunday night I passed the place. The windows were lighted and looking out at the road, but not a sound, not a footstep could I hear. I hurried my steps to get home, wondering if the old man had died.

I was sleeping peacefully near midnight, in my bed by the fire. Suddenly the cabin shook with bellowing. "Con Cregan! Con, I say, open the door. I want you!" came the loud voice of Peter McCabe; and he was knocking at the cabin door till it shook. My father unbolted it.

"Oh, it's Peter," he said. "What's the matter? Is your father worse?"

And worse he was, as it seemed, for he had been dead over an hour. My father did what he could to cheer the son up, but Peter McCabe kept talking about his father's not leaving a will. I pretended to be asleep and I snored loudly where I lay. I soon realized that it was not grief that was troubling Peter McCabe; it was greed. And my father, Con Cregan, I could tell, knew it also. They kept talking in low tones over near the fire where I could hear every word.

"I want you to help me in this business," Peter McCabe said. "Here's five guineas in gold, if you do as I bid you. You know you were always reckoned the image of my father. Before he took sick, you were mistaken for each other every day of the week. It's many a time I've seen a man go up to my father and greet him by the name of Con Cregan, you've always been so alike."

For some reason this seemed to frighten my father. He backed away a bit, and I could hear only part of what they said.

". . . You're going to pretend to be my father and want badly to make your will before you die. Then I'll send for Billy Scanlan, the schoolmaster. You can tell him what to write down in the will, leaving all the farm and everything to me, you understand. And the neighbors will see you and they'll hear your own voice. It'll never be believed by anyone that it wasn't he himself that did it."

My father said this, and my father said that. But the sight of the gold piece was too much for him, and after a while they were talking only about the details. "The room will be as dark as you please, have no fear," said Peter McCabe. "Nobody will dare to come near the bed. And my poor father, rest his soul, never learned how to write, so you need only to make an X under the name. . . ."

My father lost no time then. He just wrapped his big coat around him and slipped on his boots. He left the house while I listened for his footsteps. And when they were all gone, I set out after the two of them to watch the performance.

Things had begun when I got to the cottage. I sat outside at the window, that had only one pane of glass, and that broken.

There was a big dark room showing, with a bed at one end and a table nearby that was full of medicine bottles. Mr. Scanlan, the schoolmaster, had a lot of writing things about him, and the pen was in his hand. The country people were all around the walls, two or three deep, and hardly daring to breathe aloud while Peter McCabe went around trying to smother his grief. The half-lighted room had a misty distance in it, and everyone there seemed solemn and excited. The heavy breathing broke into a little sob when one of the people there remembered some lost friend of his own. I can tell you, it was all so real and awful that I forgot the whole thing was staged and a fake. I stood there peering through the broken window and I was shaking with fear. In the dead, low silence the buzzing of a fly was loud. I heard a faint cough from the far corner where the bed stood and that made it seem even more quiet.

Then a voice came from the bed, very weak. "Where's Billy Scanlan? I want to make my will. . . ."

"Here, father," said Peter McCabe, leading Mr. Scanlan by the hand to a place not too near the bedside.

"Write what I bid you, Billy, and be quick," said my father, Con Cregan, in his weak voice, "for I haven't a long time here afore me."

All through the room there was a sad chorus of "Oh, musha, musha!"

"I die in peace with all my neighbors and mankind," said my father; and the chorus sounded again.

"To my son Peter—and never was there a better son or a finer boy—did you write that down, Mr. Scanlan? I give all of my two big farms, with the good meadows behind Lynch's house, the forge, and grazing rights on the Dooran bog. I give him Lanty Cassern's acre, and the Luary field with the furnace—with the lime kiln—and that reminds me! Me mouth is dry as dry—just let me taste what you have in that jug, Mr. Scanlan!"

The dying man took a very hearty pull at the jug now and seemed refreshed enough to get himself past the lime kiln. His voice got louder and he began to talk faster.

"Where was I, Mr. Scanlan?" he asked. "Oh, yes. The lime kiln. Well, and I leave him—that's my fine son, Peter, I mean—I leave him the two potato gardens at Noonan's Well, and oh, it's fine, elegant crops that grow there—"

Peter was getting a bit jumpy at the sudden vigor my father showed as the punch went to his head. "Father darling, aren't you getting a bit weak?" he asked.

"That I am, Peter, my son," says Con Cregan, getting up to his elbow. "I *am* getting weak. So just touch my lip again with the jug—there's a good lad. Ah, Peter, Peter, ye've watered the drink!"

"Indeed, no, my poor father," Peter answered. "It's the taste that's leaving your mouth!" And everyone in that cabin murmured in pity for the poor dying man.

"Well, I'm near done now," says my father Con Cregan. "And there's only one little piece of land remaining. Peter, I want you to mind my last words. Are you listening? Are the neighbors listening? Is Billy Scanlan listening?"

"We're all minding," they say.

"Well, then," says my father, "It's my last will—give me over the jug—," and here he takes the longest pull of all. "And may the liquor be poison to me, if I am not just as anxious about this as about any other part of my will. I say,

I give my little land at the crossroads to poor Con Cregan; he has a heavy charge, and he is as honest and hard-working as any man I know. Be a friend to him, Peter dear, nor ever let him want while you have it yourself. If he should ever ask you for a trifle, think o' me on my deathbed. Have you got that down there, Billy Scanlan? The two acres at the crossroads to Con Cregan and his heirs forever. Ah, but I feel my poor heart lighter after that," says my father. "For a good work makes an easy conscience: and now I'll drink all the company's good health and many happy returns. And we'll drink—"

It was all Peter McCabe could do to hurry out his guests. "We must let him die in peace, good people," he said loudly, to drown out the lively voice on the bed.

And when they were all gone out at last, "Con" he said sharply to my father who was putting on his boots in the corner. "Con, ye did fine! But sure, that was a joke about the two acres at the crossroads!"

"Of course it was, Peter," my father answered. "And for that matter wasn't it all a joke, and won't the neighbors laugh hearty tomorrow when I tell them all about it!"

"Ye couldn't betray me," said Peter trembling. And after a bit he held out his hand. "Very well, Con. A bargain's a bargain. But you're a deep fellow."

And my father slipped quietly home over the bog, very well satisfied with the bit of land he'd left himself.

That's how we came to be the owners of that peculiar little plot, which is known to this day as Con's Acre.

Peter Goldthwaite's Treasure

Nathaniel Hawthorne

Nathaniel Hawthorne, American novelist (1804–1864)
Nathaniel Hawthorne was descended from seamen and
merchants at Salem, Massachusetts. He was a careful
writer, rather retiring, though very pleasant to those who
knew him. In his novels and short stories there is little
of blood and thunder. A great deal of meaning and a
wealth of suggestive thought can be seen as he turns the
events of his story over and over in his clear, precise
words. He acted as United States consul in London for
a time and lived part of his life in Rome.

It was a chill November evening. The ancient wooden
house seemed to creak in the wind. Worn and shabby, its
gables stretched up to the sky, crying "Old! Old! Old! and
decayed," out over the whole street. Twenty years of prosperity had passed by the house and its owner together. The
town was busy and thriving, while Peter Goldthwaite and his
house grew old and decayed.

In the battered kitchen there was a little fire going—just
enough, perhaps, to show how deeply the autumn chill had
crept into the timbers everywhere.

"No! No!" Goldthwaite was saying. "You will have to
find another place for the stores and offices you want to

build, John. This place is not for sale. Next summer I am going to cut the house down to its cellar. Then I will build a splendid mansion here—the whole town will be proud of it."

Old Peter Goldthwaite bent over the stove. His bones, thin and loose, seemed to crave the heat, though it did him little good when he got it. His bright little eyes peered past the sharp, hooked nose, out to the shadowy figure who sat across the table. Mr. Brown, it was, a prosperous business man who had once been Peter's partner.

Mr. Brown looked at him sadly. "It was windy schemes like this, Peter, that made us break our partnership. Do you never wonder why I have grown comfortable and prosperous, while your house and you have remained—"

"Stop! I don't want to hear about that," old Peter interrupted, his voice raised almost to a chirp in anger. "You will see when the new house is built that it is better than your ugly stores, your lawyers' offices—"

Mr. Brown rose to leave. "I hope you will be happy with your castles in the air, Peter," he said. "After all, you don't have to buy land for those, nor bricks, nor timbers! Only I sometimes wonder how you get along."

Peter shot him a glance full of suspicion. "Never mind, John," he said. "You needn't think of me at all. I have wonderful ideas—wonderful! Just get along if you're anxious. Good-bye, John! Good-bye!"

He hurried his old partner out as though there were important secrets, as though the creaking old house were full of the liveliest business. And only after the door had closed again could one notice another person in the kitchen, a little woman of about 60, who sat mending one of his two pairs of stockings. She was Tabitha Porter, who had kept house there for more than 50 years, since she had been sent there from the poorhouse.

"It is time at last!" the old gentleman said, striding excitedly up and down the kitchen. "We need to be poor no longer. It is time to find the treasure. My grandfather left it in this house, right in these walls somewhere! I have heard of it again and again. Now it is time to get it and use it. They said my grandfather, or my great-uncle, was it? was an alchemist—a magician—that the treasure was his from Old Scratch, and he himself could never touch it! A hoard of precious money—hidden right in these walls somewhere, money enough to buy food and fuel, to pay for this land we are on, to build our new mansion! Money enough—if we can only find it!"

"Best begin the work in the morning when you are fresher for it, Mr. Peter," old Tabitha advised him drily. "And leave the kitchen till the last." And all night long Peter Goldthwaite's dreams were shining with secret vaults, with gold coins and silver dishes.

Morning found the attic dust-ridden and echoing with the tearing of boards, the ripping of the saw, and the pounding of the hammer. Ancient parchment and dusty clothing, battered machinery and old trunks saw the light, and were promptly hacked to pieces. Eagerly, Peter chopped at the walls. Eagerly, Tabitha took away the rubbish. "Good! Good! she cried up to him. "A few more sticks and we shall have enough to heat the tea kettle!"

For the whole day Peter worked, and at nightfall there was plenty of wood for the fire. Panels and mouldings that were centuries old burned fierce and hot in the kitchen. Here they sat, and Peter begged the old woman to remember anything she could about his great-uncle who had hidden the treasure—anything that would help him find it. And suddenly old memories began stirring in Tabitha, and she spoke.

"Right here—right here where we are sitting," she said, "I remember another old woman like myself—but I was only a child then. She must have been a hundred years old. And she sat right here, talking to a man like yourself—thin, and tall and stooped—very much like you to look at, Mr. Peter. Why, now I think of it—it could almost be yourself she was talking to, Mr. Peter—a man bent and anxious, and forever dreaming about something. But the treasure—now they say that for the treasure the old man turned over this house to Old Scratch himself. And no sooner did he give over the deed, when the chest flew open itself and the man looked in. There was gold all over the bottom of it, they said. But when he picked it up out of the chest, it turned into old rags right in his hand—old and dusty rags, like these out of the attic."

Mr. Peter thought nothing at all of the story. Next day his ax and hammer were busier than ever. Down on the second floor there were rooms once used by Governor Dudley with charcoal sketches all over the walls, picturing the ancient glories of the house. One queer sketch showed a ragged man digging frantically into the earth. Behind him, the devil peered over his shoulder watching every spadeful. Under this sketch there was a secret compartment. It had nothing in it, except an old brass lamp and some mysterious writing that no one could read.

"It's in your own hand, Mr. Peter! See, that's the way you yourself write!" Tabitha exclaimed, and burst out laughing. But that was impossible, really, because the wall had been plastered over and sealed long before Peter Goldthwaite was born.

Peter felt a little dazed. He carried the lamp over to the window, to think things out. "This lamp ought to light something up," he thought. But as he looked out at the late January day he saw only icicles on the housetops, melting into millions of sparkling drops under the sunlight. He saw the white snow, packed solid as white marble. Sleigh bells jingled and light carts skimmed the snow, and now and then the big stagecoach whirled through the tangled traffic. There were rosy cheeks and wholesome faces. There was a babble of voices. And there was the gaunt figure looking down upon all this from his battered and rusty casement.

"What the blazes are you doing there, Peter?" some one called to him from below. It was Mr. Brown, his old partner. "I hear such a racket whenever I pass by! Are you repairing the old house—or building a new one?"

"Too late! Too late for that!" Peter answered, hastily

shutting the window. Trembling, he began his work again. There was a rusty old key that he found in a chink in the wall. With this he found another treasure, a bottle of old wine and some few odd coins and a medal. For days there was nothing else—only sticks to light the fire. The house stood at last with nothing in it, an empty shell stripped down to the kitchen. And when a snowstorm tugged at the empty walls, they creaked and swayed dangerously. The whole house had been eaten and had passed in smoke up its own chimney.

"The treasure must be in this kitchen then!" Peter exclaimed, as though he had already found it. "We have only to pull it out now!" And he was so excited at the idea that he opened the wine bottle and filled glasses for himself and Tabitha. "It is as good as found!" he said, drinking a goblet.

All this time Mr. Brown had been wondering and worrying about Peter Goldthwaite. So he decided to brave the storm and look in on him. Wrapped in his cloak and comforters and scarves, he approached the place—how ominously it was creaking and rattling and groaning in the wind! The door was open, and there was nothing inside. Darkness! Carefully he walked through and pushed open the kitchen door.

Peter and Tabitha had their backs to the door. They were crouched over a big chest that had been dragged out of a great hole in the chimney. The old woman held a lamp, which cast its light upon iron clasps and clamps and iron plates studded with iron nailheads—strength enough there to withstand the centuries! With the key flourished in his hand, Peter was exclaiming over their find, while Tabitha begged that for mercy's sake he should turn the key and look inside. Mr. Brown came forward to see as the great lid swung back. But there was no shining gold there. There was only a dark interior and parchments yellow with age, strange treasury notes, bills, and parchment money, printed before the American Revolution.

"What does this mean? What is it? Tell me what it is, John," Peter begged, his voice trembling with eagerness.

"This must be the treasure you hunted for," Brown said

quietly. "But you can never spend it, Peter, because the banks and governments that printed it have long since gone out of existence. This is money issued before the United States began. When the Colonies came together in the Revolution, they printed their own money. The old bills and money, printed earlier, began to have less and less value. And your ancestor bought up all this paper and hid it away, thinking it would become valuable again when the Revolution failed. Only the Revolution did not fail, Peter. You remember that the Colonies got together—and they stayed together as the United States of America! Their money became the money of the whole country. And this paper—these parchments of failure and isolation—it was these that lost all their value. But never mind, Peter. This is still the right kind of money for you—for your castles in the air!"

Peter Goldthwaite huddled nearer the fire. His whole frame seemed to shiver as the house shook dangerously under the force of the wind outside. He folded his arms, and sat upon the chest that held so safely his poor useless treasure. "I must die here, John," he said. "You and Tabitha go at once, before the house caves in. I—I have been a fool, and I must wait for what comes now."

John Brown began laughing heartily. "Nonsense, my friend Peter," he said merrily. "There is nothing to die for. The town has grown well in spite of your schemes, and the land under this house is now worth a great deal. And until I can sell it and give you the money to start over again, there is plenty of room in my house for you and Tabitha. There will even be a place there for your treasure chest."

"Why—why, that's wonderful," Peter exclaimed, up at a bound. "And I have a wonderful new plan, too! Why, I can take all the money I get for the land, and with it—"

"Yes, Peter," John said. "I am sure of that. But I have an even better plan. I shall have the court appoint a guardian for you, to keep your money safely as you will never do. Then you will have it as you need it. And if you want to gamble, my friend, you need only open this chest of yours, and you can go as far as you like—with Peter Goldthwaite's treasure!"

Edward Randolph's Portrait

Nathaniel Hawthorne

With a long, cold evening ahead of me, and the gas light flaring from the street lamps, I drew a chair to the fire beside old Mr. Tiffany's, asking my host to draw a glass apiece of punch for us. There it was, steaming hot—a slice of lemon below, the dark-red port wine at the surface, and a sprinkling of nutmeg: nothing better for loosening the tongue and bringing old stories to the surface.

The Province House—yes, a good deal of our colonial history took place there; and it was not long before Mr. Tiffany was telling me a choice bit of it—of the ancient Government Randolph and his more recent successor, Lieutenant Governor Hutchinson, who had occupied the Province House before the Boston Massacre.

There is an ancient picture over the mantelpiece of one room in the Province House. Time has worn down the paint to a cloudy blackness. None of the features is distinguishable. Above it, there are relics of black draperies that once had been used to conceal the painted features. But these had long since grown unnecessary, as time blurred the outlines and hid the painted form. Why the painting had been concealed when it was still clear, why it still hung there though it was long since only a black blur, no one could say. But hang there it did and no one dared to disturb it. Gently, old Mr. Tiffany told me the story.

Relations between the Colonies and Great Britain were now at the breaking point. Three regiments of the king's troops had just arrived by transport, and they were to be quartered upon the resentful citizens of Boston. But the Bostonians would sooner have quartered them dead than alive. They hated to have foreign troops lodged among them. Resentment at this latest attack upon liberty and privacy by the foreign king was now general. That their homes should be invaded so that the king's tyranny could flourish in their free colony—that seemed to them intolerable.

Intolerable it seemed also to the young cousin of the governor, Captain Francis Lincoln, of Castle William, where a great many of the soldiers were to be placed. It was intolerable also to the governor's young niece, Alice Vane, a delicate and talented young lady, who had been educated in Italy, yet was still strongly Colonial in her sympathy.

In the Province House both these young people watched Lieutenant Governor Hutchinson as he sat in thought, staring at the darkened canvas before him. Alice became curious about the mysterious painting. She herself had some skill in the art and had learned a great deal in Italy. Was this some respected masterpiece, she asked, ruined, but still kept for its memory?

Captain Lincoln looked gravely at the picture. "Nothing is known of the painter," he said, "and little enough of the subject. But there are many wild tales and fantasies about it. They say that it is the very likeness of the Evil One, taken at a witch meeting near Salem. Its true resemblance to Satan was stated long ago by several convicted wizards and witches.

"In the blackness of that picture, it is said, the demon himself still lurks. And when a public calamity is about to take place, his face peers forth and is again visible. And this face, as legend tells, Governor Shirley once saw before the shameful and bloody defeat of General Abercrombie at Ticonderoga. Servants are said to have glimpsed it in the dead of night. Though if any was bold enough to hold a torch close to it, the features disappeared. One of the oldest inhabitants of Boston says that his father once saw—"

He stopped as he saw Alice shudder. "The reality could not be so bad as the legend," she said. "Perhaps it would pay to restore the picture and clear away the darkness both of the story and the canvas."

Here a smile lighted the face of the Lieutenant Governor. There was an unusual doubt in his voice as he spoke. "I—I know well the subject of that portrait. He is—Sir Edward Randolph, the founder of this house."

The young captain was startled. "Not that Edward Randolph who earned the hatred of all the colonies by repealing the first charter under which our ancestors enjoyed real liberty? Surely, not the archenemy of New England!" he cried.

"The same—the same Randolph, whose unhappy lot it was to know the hatred of the mob," answered the older man.

But the captain was not to be put off. "That Edward Randolph who was cursed by his own people, till the face of wretchedness he wore was too melancholy and terrible to look upon! If this was his picture, then it is no wonder it was permitted to hide under its merciful blackness of time!"

"There are worse things than the hatred of the mob," said the lieutenant governor, gazing at his niece. "The rebuke of a king is more to be dreaded than the clamor of the multitude.

"Captain Lincoln, I have made up my mind. You must give up the fortress of Castle William to the British troops. The other two regiments will be lodged in the 'town or camp upon the Common. It is time our rebellion gave way to loyalty to the king's troops."

With this startling decision, undreamt of by any loyal colonist, Lieutenant Governor Hutchinson left the room, and never answered the protests of his young relatives. As the young lady rose to leave, she glanced up at the wall and regarded the somber painting there.

"This is your hour. Come forth, dark, evil shape," she said, and a strange smile was on her lips.

That evening, in the same room, Lieutenant Governor Hutchinson, ruler of the colony in the absence of the governor, met with the members of his council. And with them were those honest and frank old gentlemen, the Selectmen of Boston. These were men of the people, stern Puritans of New England.

There between silver candlesticks on his desk lay the order of occupation which Hutchinson had decided to sign. With what warmth and feeling was the chairman of the Selectmen pleading with his ruler!

"Think, sir, while there is time!" he cried. "Let no blood eternally stain Your Honor's memory. Let history remember you as a patriot, as an upright ruler. . . . Do not give way to the tyranny of England!"

"Enough!" cried Hutchinson. "It is not the praise of the mob I seek, but of the lawful king, whose banner you may one day live to honor more, when you seek its protection. Rabble-rousers may raise the Devil; but *we* should not ask for his approval!"

"Let no evil spirit enter your words," answered the ancient Selectman. "We will strive with prayer against the oppressor and submit to a wise Providence—only after our best efforts to change our lot!"

There was no mistaking these words. The Puritan was near to outright resistance. Governor Hutchinson seized his pen to confirm the king's order. A hush had fallen in expectation of the fateful scratching—when, in that silence, a hand was stretched forth.

What insolence! Young Captain Lincoln had dared to stop his cousin, the lieutenant governor. But he only pointed mutely at the portrait. The sable curtain was once more over the canvas. With a bitter smile, Alice Vane glided toward it, and she held back the obscuring velvet.

Surprise and horror broke from every tongue when she

had done so. There, there, vivid and stern before them, was the face of Edward Randolph. If his spirit had come from the place of torment to astonish them, he could not have worn more of the terrors of hell upon his features as they glared forth from the frame.

"Providence for a wise purpose has dissolved the mist of years. Behold your warning!" said the Selectman.

The half-length portrait of a figure in ancient ruff and embroidered velvet seemed to glare wickedly at the spectators. It started from its background as if projected by some hideous guilt, the withering scorn of mankind, the weight of a great shame. As though the clouds of years had parted, the curse that lay on those features was visible. "It—it would drive me mad," Hutchinson whispered.

"He trampled upon a people's rights," said Alice. "Behold his punishment and be warned."

But the spell was broken. The lieutenant governor turned in anger upon his niece. "Do you think that with your Italian tricks, your stage effects, your painter's arts, you can alter the destiny of our nation? See how I am influenced by the spirits you raise to frighten me! Though that senseless picture should cry, 'Forbear!' it could not move me." And with a scribble of desperation and anger, he signed his name, and shuddered.

"It is done!" he whispered.

"May heaven forgive the deed," said Alice Vane.

Next morning there were many conflicting stories of the picture. But the fact everyone agreed on was this: that the dark cloud that had hidden it had settled again upon the canvas, and no one could see a painting where the frightful figure had appeared. Perhaps Alice's renewing process was only temporary, but many claimed that the evil spirit had merely withdrawn itself again.

After a short while, whoever looked into the face of Hutchinson seemed strangely to recollect the portrait that had appeared for a moment; and he trembled as if he had seen a spirit. The lieutenant governor himself, when he died beyond the ocean some years later, cried out that he was choked by the blood of the Boston Massacre. And Francis Lincoln, who stood beside him at the death, saw in his tortured face a close likeness to the frantic features of Edward Randolph. Perhaps, at the last hour, he felt with added keenness the weight of the curse.

* * *

"Is there nothing on this mysterious canvas now," I asked Mr. Tiffany, "to bear witness in this strange story?"

"Some day an historian may study it," he answered, "and find evidence of what I have said, in the dark pigments."

But the winter wind, whistling in the rooms above us, reminded me at last of the night and of the journey I still had to make. It sounded through the upper portions of the house, as though the echoes of half a century were reviving in the ancient rooms above us. Ghostly voices still murmured in my ear as I walked down the doorsteps and fought my way homeward against the drifting snowstorm, with the dark picture still in my mind—the twisted features of Governor Randolph always before me.

The Devil and Tom Walker

Washington Irving

Washington Irving, American essayist (1783–1859) Direct, blunt speech was not for Washington Irving. His talent was in the beautiful style and the elegantly-turned phrase. At first he was a lawyer, but soon he became known as an essayist, story writer and historian. Something of a diplomat, he became Secretary of the United States Legation in London, and Minister to Spain. His "Knickerbocker's History of New York" is the earliest American humorous work of literary pretensions.

New England in the year 1727 was visited by a series of violent earthquakes. They had some value, of course, because there were a good many hardened sinners at the time who simply would not repent. With the earthquakes, some of them were shaken from their evil ways, and that was a blessing.

But the miserly, cheating Tom Walker, and that miserly scold, his wife, would not repent. They were a precious pair of frauds who lived near a great dark marsh outside of Boston, on the bank of an inlet. Gigantic oaks and hemlocks stretched gaunt arms across the treacherous swampland. In fact, if legend were to be believed, Captain Kidd himself had cached quite a hoard under one of those very trees.

The region abounded with tales of how the devil himself

had directed the burial of this particular treasure—just as he directed, no doubt, every such treasure. But Tom Walker and his wife thought little of such matters. They were more actively engaged in squeezing a living out of a few miserable hens, a sick horse or two—woefully mistreated—and the scraggly land. Or else they were fighting with each other so loudly and bitterly that the tumble-down house, the neglected land and the whole forbidding place were avoided by the neighbors.

It chanced one day that Tom Walker was coming home through the swamp, ignoring the tangling pines and hemlocks overhead, whose great branches made night out of the noonday; and avoiding the pits and marshes and the green standing pools. He stepped from tuft to tuft of dry land like a cat and thought nothing of arousing the water snakes or owls till he came to rest near an old Indian fort. Here the Indians had made sacrifices and prayers to the evil spirit; here the people of the region seldom or never ventured; and here just at dusk Tom Walker sat himself down to rest.

He poked his staff into the black earth and heard the call of the tree-toads. Some hard object lay in the earth under his staff, he felt. In a moment, he had it to the surface—a split skull it was, with an Indian tomahawk deep in it.

"Humph!" said Tom Walker, kicking the dirt off it.

"Let that skull alone!" said a voice behind him. Tom was quite startled. No one had made a sound there. But an enormous man was sitting down beside him on the stump of a tree. The stranger was swarthy and grimy—neither white nor black nor red—his complexion not downright black nor copper-colored, but smudged as if he had worked all day at a forge. There was an ax on his shoulder, and his eyes were an angry red as he spoke.

"What are you doing on my grounds?" asked this stranger with a hoarse voice.

"Your grounds?" sneered Tom. "Why they're no more yours than mine. They belong to Deacon Peabody."

"Deacon Peabody!" growled the stranger. "Let him look more to *his* sins and less to his neighbors'. Look yonder and see how Deacon Peabody is faring!"

The pointing finger showed a tall straight tree reaching nobly upward. But the core of it was rotten, and the ax had nearly cut it through. The first high wind would certainly carry it down. And the name of Deacon Peabody, who had thrived so well on his hard bargains made with the Indians, was carved upon that tree. Looking around further, Tom observed now that every great tree bore some name upon it. The one on which he had been seated, evidently just cut down, was Crowninshield's. The man, it was whispered about town, had made his money by piracy. Tom looked hard at the stranger.

"And who are you, if I may be so bold?" he asked.

"I go by various names—the wild huntsman, the strange miner. Around here I am called the dark woodsman. The Indians used to oblige me now and then by roasting a settler here."

"Well, then, the long and the short of it is that you're Old Scratch himself," said Tom, sturdily. Long years with his wife had made him confident in any company.

"The same, at your service!" replied the stranger.

And that was the beginning of their negotiations which are still the talk of the neighborhood. Tom Walker was promised some of Captain Kidd's treasure if he would use it exactly as he was told. The bargain was the usual one offered, but even Tom Walker, wicked as he was, could not decide to close the deal on the spot, but only promised to think it over. And the devil left his fingerprint on Tom's forehead, to prove his identity.

When he came home, Tom noticed that there was a black mark on his brow that nothing would take off; and he read in the paper that Absalom Crowninshield had just died. These two facts together convinced him that the meeting with the devil was a real one. And so disturbed did he grow in spirit, that he told his wife the whole story—even the part about offering him the hidden treasure.

At once she wanted him to seal the bargain and sell his soul. It is true that Tom had wanted to do this himself, but he refused flatly as soon as he heard her suggest it. So his wife decided to make her own deal with the devil. The first time she went, the stranger was sulky and she told Tom she had to return with an offering.

And so she did, taking the silver teapot, spoons, and all Tom's other valuables. But she never returned.

For a long time Tom thought it over. He had lost his property, it was true. But his wife was gone, and his relief at this fact made him bolder. He also felt something like gratitude for the old villain. So he set out for the swamp again, determined to find the devil and seal the bargain.

That shrewd businessman finally appeared, swinging his ax idly and humming a tune, till Tom was sure he cared nothing for the bargain. He insisted that Tom use all the money for the slave traffic. But even Tom's wickedness would not permit this. So they finally compromised and made Tom a money lender, which he was well content to be. And of course the devil set down, in addition, the usual price he demands for his favors. That very night, Tom would go to Boston and open up shop. In his enthusiasm, he even offered to drive his customers, whenever he could, to the devil.

Tom Walker made a very fine business of it, too. There had been a great rage for speculating just before this time—new settlements, cities in the wilderness, projects for land that no one could locate. Then the fever subsided and the imaginary fortunes vanished. Everyone needed money and thought he could pay it back in a few days. There was little thought about the security. The needy, the adventurous, the gambling man, the thriftless tradesman, the merchant without credit—all put whatever they had left into Tom Walker's waiting hands in order to get a little ready cash. And his terms were harder according to the need they were in.

In a very short time, Tom Walker was rich and mighty. Out of vanity, he built himself an enormous house. But he left the job unfinished and unfurnished, because he hated to give up the money. His carriage was the finest in the neighborhood. But the horses were starving; and the wheels shrieked over the whole countryside whenever he rode, as if the souls of his debtors were squealing for mercy. He was too stingy to grease the axles!

As time went on, Tom grew wiser and more cautious, and he began bitterly to repent his bargain with the devil. So he took to violent righteousness. He corrected others at every chance he got—or made the chance if there didn't happen to be any. He went to church regularly, but only to chant the hymns with extraordinary loudness and fervor as if strong lungs would get him to heaven. And he wanted to review persecution of several religious sects. His zeal and devotion were praised widely.

He carried a small Bible in his coat pocket so the devil might not take him unawares and kept a great folio Bible on his countinghouse desk. Frequently his victims would come in and have to wait nearby until he'd finished reading a passage. Then he'd lay his spectacles in the place, so he couldn't lose it, and drive a perfectly savage bargain with his visitor.

One hot day, thunderous with lowering summer clouds, he sat in his white linen cap and dressing gown, foreclosing a mortgage against an unlucky friend of his, while the man sat there pleading pitifully for his future and his family.

"Charity begins at home," Tom Walker said. "I must take care of myself in these hard times."

"But you have made so much money from me," said the man.

"May the devil take me if I've made a cent on this whole transaction!"

At this, three loud knocks sounded, and Tom stepped out to see who it was. There was a great black man standing outside, holding a black horse that was stamping with impatience.

"Tom, you're come for," the man said. It was too late to retreat. The little Bible was inside, in the pocket of his coat. The big Bible lay on the desk, hidden under the mortgage he was going to foreclose. The grimy man whisked him into the saddle, lashed the horse, and away they galloped into the midst of a thunderstorm. The clerks stuck their pens on their ears and stared at their master galloping off, his white cap bobbing, his dressing gown fluttering in the wind, and sparks shooting off from the horse's hoofs. In the distance, they looked now as if they galloped out of sight. They disappeared, as though they were sinking gradually into the earth as they rode.

Tom Walker never returned to foreclose his mortgage, but the clattering of hoofs along the road was reported from many places during the fierce thunderstorm that raged. And some reported a figure like Tom's, mounted and galloping toward the marshes, into the black hemlock swamp near the old Indian fort, and it was shrieking for mercy. And these people told also that they had seen a thunderbolt fall at the fort. It seemed to set the whole forest in a blaze. Then the figures were gone.

Trustees of Tom Walker's estate tried to sell his property, but they came across a curious trouble in their work. When they searched his files, they found his mortgages and bonds burnt down to cinders. Then they opened the iron chest that had held his gold and silver. There was nothing but chips and shavings. His horses were gone, too. Only two skeletons lay in his stables. And the next day the stable and the house itself, dry as tinder, burned down to the ground.

If anyone doubts this story, or refuses to accept its lesson—that greed and ill-gotten wealth are hard bought, you have only to explore that region. The hole under the oak tree, from which Captain Kidd's treasure was taken, may still be seen there; and the swamp around it and the Indian fort are haunted on stormy nights by a figure on horseback that wears a white cap and a dressing gown.

The story has given rise to a proverb or popular saying in New England: "The Devil and Tom Walker," which is still used as a dire warning to usurers.

The Specter Bridegroom
Washington Irving

The Baron von Landshort had great wealth. He had an ancient and imposing castle. And he had a young and attractive daughter.

Attractive, did I say? Ah, you should have heard the young Count von Altenburg tell about her. She was beautiful. She was talented. She understood the deep art of embroidery. She could even read a little, and spell out her name without missing a letter—large and clear, so her aunts could read it without spectacles! She had learned all this in only 18 years. And besides, she was quiet, and well-behaved, and graceful, and obedient, and—

All this the Count von Altenburg kept telling his friend, Herman von Starkenfaust. He told him and told him and told him. Only, about the third or fourth time he told him, as they rode on together through the forest, von Altenburg had the idea that perhaps Herman had stopped listening. Amazing! How could Herman stop listening, when the young count could hardly talk fast enough to tell all about her? Why, he hadn't even told him that—

"Look, my dear Count," said Herman von Starkenfaust, "we must not forget, after all, that you have never even seen the lady. Your father arranged—"

"Of course! And it is said in Landshort that when she goes out for a walk—"

"And, my dear Count," Herman went on patiently, "neither has she ever had the pleasure of seeing you."

"That is true," said the count. "But—"

"And perhaps you should remember that for us Starkenfausts—for my family, remember—there is nothing fine about any of the Landshorts. They have been our enemies for generations. I am sure she is an excellent person, my dear Count, but just as soon as we are through the dangerous passes of these woods—as soon as I know that you are safely past the robbers who are always lurking here in the Oldenwald—then I must leave you to go on to your wedding. You cannot invite me to the castle of Landshort, and I—I cannot accept!"

By this time both the men were a little excited and had ridden on far in advance of their followers. So that when, a moment later, a band of armed robbers swarmed out of the woods with drawn swords, they had to fight alone for a few minutes, against great odds, too. Their soldiers came up at last, and the robbers fled in panic. But the young Count von Altenburg was no longer on his horse. They found him upon the ground, mortally wounded.

They brought him to a friar's hut and tried to tend him, but it was too late. "Herman! Herman!" he called to his friend before dying. "I must keep my appointment with her. Somehow I must keep my appointment." Tears welled up in his friend's eyes, and he shook his head sadly.

"I see," the count muttered. "Then you must go and explain what has happened! You must go and keep it for me—"

"How can I?" asked Herman.

"I shall not lie in my grave! I shall not lie quietly if you do not go for me, Herman!" the count cried. And to soothe him at the last, Herman von Starkenfaust took his hand and made a solemn pledge that he would travel to Landshort and fulfill his friend's promise to the famous beauty.

Meanwhile, the castle of the Baron von Landshort was busy as a hive. The servants worked at top speed, stopping only to hear their master's cries of "Hurry! Hurry!" Poor relatives sat at the baron's table and roared with laughter every time he made a joke. The daughter looked fresh and lovely, and her aunts quarrelled so heatedly over everything she was supposed to wear for the wedding, that she could finally dress exactly as she pleased. Wine and venison loaded the tables. As the hours passed and no one arrived, the baron climbed up to his highest tower and watched the roads.

Peasants were coming home, tired from their work. Sometimes a lone traveler crossed the horizon in another direction. Distant horns floated in across the valley. But the Count von Altenburg did not appear. Bats flitted out against the gathering dusk. Roads melted off against the earth and the trees, and the sun had long since set. But the Count von Altenburg did not appear.

The wedding meats were long overcooked. The cook was tearing his hair. The guests wandered around hungry. The baron had almost ordered that the meal be served, when he heard the long blast of a horn echoing against the castle walls. The drawbridge was slowly lowered, and there before the gate stood a stranger, mounted on a black steed. He was pale and melancholy. His eyes glowed strangely in the darkness, and he said never a word.

The baron, uncomfortable and annoyed because his son-in-law came there alone and without followers, made a great fuss and talked loudly and rapidly. Several times the stranger opened his mouth to speak. Just as often, the baron's hearty courtesy made it impossible to hear a word. The inner court, where the ladies appeared to greet him, found the same scene. There was a great clatter of greeting, questions and comments, and no chance for the stranger to answer.

But when the bride came forward, then the stranger stood in reverent silence. He looked at her, his whole soul in his eyes. And she too could only glance at him shyly, and say nothing, though a faint smile played quietly upon her lips.

"It is late!" the baron cried, "and our guests are waiting. No time for talk and explanations!" And he hustled everyone to the feast. They sat down under the jousting-spears hung on the walls, under the tattered battle banners, and the mounted heads of wolves and boars staring down at the merriment. Everyone was joyous. But those who noticed the bridegroom saw that no food passed his lips the whole evening. No laughter came from his lips at the loud jokes echoing across the table. All he did was to speak softly and sadly to the ear of the maiden.

Through the roaring songs, the cloudy mood of the bridegroom seemed to influence the bride. Once or twice she seemed to tremble a little as she listened, and anxious whispers began to go from guest to guest as they noticed. Gradually, laughter became rarer at the table. Wild stories and legends replaced the jokes that had made everything merry earlier. The baron himself began to tell of a goblin horseman, who came and carried off a fair maiden. So real did it seem, that several of the ladies shrieked, and the baron himself paused in awe at his own story.

Somehow it seemed to the baron that the bridegroom listening to him had grown taller. In a moment, he saw the youth rising strangely and stalking toward the courtyard.

"Going? Going away at midnight?" the baron cried, his words ringing strangely across the great chamber. "But your room upstairs is ready for you, if you wish—"

"Tonight I must lay my head in a different room," the figure cast back over his shoulder. A chill came upon the baron. He followed to the courtyard. There was the great black horse of the stranger, and it pawed at the earth impatiently, tossing its head up toward the high vaulted roof.

Now the figure turned to the baron. "We are alone, and I may speak," he said gravely, and his word echoed across the court. "I have a solemn promise, and no one else may fulfill it. At the Wurtzburg Cathedral, where I am awaited—there I must go now."

"But not till tomorrow!" cried the baron. "Your bride will be there tomorrow. You will meet her for the wedding."

"No bride—no bride expects me there," said the stranger. "Only the worms—the worms expect me. For my body now lies at Wurtzburg, where I am a dead man, and at midnight I am to be buried. I am a dead man, and the worms expect me!" And in a moment, the clatter of horse's hoofs was sounding in the distance and blending with the night wind, and the stranger was there no longer.

Inside the castle there was great doubt and wonder at all this. Many of the guests thought the baron had merely drunk a bit too deeply. But next day word arrived that the young Count von Altenburg had really been slain on the road and his body buried at the Cathedral. Then the tale of the ghost spread far and wide.

One of the aunts, who slept with her niece for safety, looked out of her window one night and saw the figure of the stranger outside, mounted on his black horse, the moonlight streaming down upon him. And the terrified aunt would sleep there no longer.

A few days later, the bride herself disappeared. Two of the servants swore they had heard the clatter of a horse's hoofs galloping off at midnight. The castle was searched and hunting parties sent out to every path and glen in the Odenwald. The baron was in despair. All the fearful tales of the wild region were revived, and told, and told again, with new details and terrors.

The very next morning the baron mounted his horse and was going out to help in the search, when he suddenly froze half up in his stirrup. For there was a lady riding toward him, and the specter bridegroom was with her. She was his daughter. When she came up to him, she threw herself to the ground and began to beg her father's forgiveness. The stranger, splendidly dressed, his face flushed and glowing, seemed handsome and quite real beside her.

"Who are you? Are you not a ghost?" the baron at last managed to ask him.

The stranger shook his head vigorously. "No ghost," he

said. "But I was afraid you might make me one! For my name is von Starkenfaust—a name you have quarreled with for generations. But I have no quarrel with you, Baron, no more than my poor friend had, Count von Altenburg, who was coming to marry your daughter when he was killed. I came only to tell what had happened. But I had no chance to speak, until it was too late to speak at the feast. And when I had seen your daughter—how could I speak? I could only escape as you saw, trying not to provoke your anger. And when I wooed your daughter and won her—surely, father, you will not now deny us your forgiveness!"

Well, after all—what was the use? The baron had his daughter back—and he certainly loved her dearly. And the son-in-law was handsome enough, and looked as if he might be wealthy as well. All's fair in love, he had often said himself. Family feuds, of course, are a serious matter. But it was a great relief, you know, to be sure that one's grandchildren were not going to be goblins.

So the baron granted his consent and forgiveness and a new wedding celebration again filled the castle walls with feasting and good cheer for everyone.

Peter Rugg,
the Missing Man
William Austin

William Austin, American novelist (1778–1841) William Austin led such a busy life as a civic leader and commentator that he had very little time for writing. From his youth he was resisting injustices of one sort or another. He refused to join the honor society of Phi Beta Kappa in college because he believed a classmate had not been treated well. On the famous United States ship Constitution *he became schoolmaster and chaplain in order to finance his law studies. He went into politics and held many offices. His story of "Peter Rugg" is set against a background of symbolism and authentic folklore and has been generally admired.*

The coach was crowded inside. I had to climb up and sit with the driver. We were about ten miles out of Providence when I noticed the horses. Their ears lay flat back, and they seemed nervous and disturbed.

"There'll be a storm in a moment," the driver said. "Watch out for the storm breeder."

Storm breeder? I was puzzled and uncomfortable. I looked out over the bleak countryside and shivered. There was a cloud over the horizon. There was a speck on the road, growing rapidly larger. Toward us came a great black horse drawing a light carriage with a man and a child in it. And the man kept urging his horse forward, glancing at our coach with worried looks as he sped past us and went on ahead.

My coachman looked at me oddly. "He stops just long enough to ask the way to Boston—even when we're just outside of Boston! Sometimes I don't answer him, and he just stares and stares. . . . Better have your coat on, sir. The storm comes right after him."

Sure enough, the east showed black. A dark storm cloud rolled over the turnpike, greater and more solid with every moment. In an instant it was cleft by lightning. "Did you see them—did you see the man and his child right up in the sky?" my driver demanded, shaking my arm briefly. I had seen only the cloud cleft by lightning.

At Polley's Tavern where we paused, two people had seen the same carriage on the road. The man in it had stopped and asked the way to Boston. But when the thunder rolled overhead, he had dashed on like a man possessed. A peddler said he had met the carriage often. But it was always during a rain. They were flooded with the storm, and the man never stopped for an answer anyhow, so that the peddler was glad to be rid of him.

Some years later I heard a group of men talk of the strange traveler—*Peter Rugg,* they called him.

"He is a man under judgment or trial of heaven," one of them told me. "He neither eats nor drinks nor sleeps. He seems to be looking for eternity or to find a resting place. His child looks older than he does, but his horse—"

"Yes. What about his horse?" I urged, remembering the great black beast that had passed me on the turnpike.

"The horse has gotten fatter and sleeker now for 20 years," said the man slowly. "And the man gets more bewildered. When I told him Boston was a hundred miles away, he said, 'How can you deceive me? Boston shifts with the winds. It is east, one man says; another says it is west. And the sign posts are all pointed wrong. . . .' I tried to have him stop and dry off, but 'No! no!' he cried, "I must reach home by tonight—you are wrong about the distance!" He—but look up the road: here he comes now."

I looked where the man was pointing. The same great dark, spirited horse cantered up, drawing the light carriage behind it as if it were no more than an eggshell. The strange driver reined to as I called out to him.

"Sir, are you not Mr. Rugg?" I called out. The man

looked dazed, though he spoke politely.

"Yes! Yes!" he answered. "But is this the road to Boston? I must get there soon—shall I swing off on the old road or go along the turnpike?"

"But, man!" I said. "The old road is 117 miles and the turnpike is 97!" But the man and his child, both wet and muddy, were going on. "How can you say so?" he demanded reproachfully. "It is wrong to trifle with a traveler. You know it is only 40 miles—40 miles from Newburyport to Boston."

But this was the town of Hartford. The river, I explained carefully, was the Connecticut, not the Merrimack. A thunder cloud, I saw, was coming toward us, and Rugg began to cry out piteously. "Cities are wandering, and even the rivers change their courses. We shall have a rainy night—a rainy night! Oh, that fatal oath!" And he was off with the sound of the thunder, his horse pawing at the turnpike.

There was a Mrs. Croft on Middle Street in Boston, who told me more. Peter Rugg had come to her house one day and asked to see Mrs. Rugg. The house, he said, was his own, and he recognized some old landmarks. But the people he spoke about had all been dead a long time, and it was terribly hard to make him believe that Mrs. Rugg was not there. Meanwhile his horse was pawing the earth in great impatience. He hurried back to the child waiting in his carriage, glancing back dazedly toward the house.

"How could I think this is the old town of Boston?" he muttered. "This is a much finer city—and Boston must be a great distance from here. The good woman never even heard of it. . . . No home tonight!" His voice sounded despairing, as the great steed swept off.

Peter Rugg, one old gentleman told me, had been known since the Boston Massacre in 1770. His little "child," Jenny, was about 60 years old. Prosperous and well-liked, Rugg had lived with his wife and daughter in Boston. Nobody knew anything against him, except for a violent temper which sometimes seized him. He might swear then or kick his way through a solid door that blocked him! Nothing in heaven or earth had his respect in anger.

One day Rugg and his little daughter stopped in West Cambridge at the home of a Mr. Cutter, and there a terrible tempest broke over them. Cutter urged them to stay overnight, to avoid the carriage journey in such a storm; but this only stirred up Peter Rugg's temper.

"Let the storm increase!" cried Rugg. "I will see home tonight in spite of the last tempest—or may I never see home!" And his horse reared, and off they surged into the rain. On dark stormy nights, people who knew Rugg said that they heard his heavy step outside or heard the creaking and rattling of his carriage. Often, they said, he would pass right by their doors, vainly fighting to stop his horse. He was seen driving furiously through Rhode Island or the hills of New Hampshire. But never was he seen to remain in Boston.

There was a toll bridge at Charleston, and the toll-gatherer said he had often seen the carriage pass his bridge without paying. Once in anger he rose and hurled his stool after it. The stool skidded clear across the bridge, but the carriage only faded into the darkness.

Then, in 1825, there was a racecourse in Richmond, Virginia, where two famous racehorses were running—Dart and Lightning. Suddenly a strange old-fashioned light carriage appeared on the plain behind them, drawn by a majestic black horse. In a moment it overtook the racers and passed them. It was gone before anyone knew exactly what had happened. One said it was not pulled by a horse, but by a great black ox. Others were sure it was a horse. But the tracks it left on the turf were not like those of a horse. They were cloven— broken in two.

Storms and stories followed Rugg through Delaware, Virginia, and New York before I saw him again. It was at a ferry, where I found him arguing with the ferryman. The man would not take Rugg's coin for the ferry fare. Without a word I offered Rugg an American coin for his. When I looked at the one he had given me, I saw it was English—a half crown, minted by the English parliament—the date on it was 1649. And Peter Rugg expressed great gratitude to me for the exchange, with a fine politeness, even though his horse was driving everyone on the ferry frantic. The horse kept rearing and plunging, as if it would splinter every board before we made the other shore.

The last I saw of him was at an auction of the old estate he had owned in Boston. When there were no more heirs to claim the place, the State of Massachusetts decided to sell Rugg's property, and most of the local people came in for the auction.

"You know," said the auctioneer, "that there are some people who say Peter Rugg is still alive. Wonderful man! Over 50 years ago he disappeared in a terrific storm—in a light carriage. Lively fellow! And the fact that he would now be—well, let's see—yes, over a hundred years of age!— that would hardly matter. Of course, this is a good piece of business property; and there are great names who lived right close by—James Otis, Samuel Adams, Joseph Warren, and Josiah Quincy—that would make this a valuable piece of property. So we needn't wonder that some shrewd folks might want to keep Peter Rugg alive—or at least, the story about him. Might keep the bidding down, mightn't it? Frighten some folks out of bidding for the land, maybe. Well, let's see—"

Bidding went on briskly enough, in spite of the story. But suddenly there was a rumble of thunder; and there were Peter Rugg and Jenny in their carriage, looking at the ruins.

"Our house has been burnt!" he cried. "Here are all our neighbors to help us. Only I pray your mother is safe, Jenny, I hope nothing has happened to Dame Rugg!" The hammer of the auction held still, and all eyes were on the carriage.

"But this is no fire!" Peter Rugg cried again, his face wrathful. "What are you doing here, all of you? You know me! You know I am Peter Rugg!" And still no one answered.

"But I know you well—every one of you!" Rugg went on. "There is a Winslow. You, there—you are a Sargent. And there is a Sewall. That's a Dudley next to him—why . . ."

Everyone was silent with fear and wonder; but from somewhere in the crowd I heard a voice.

"There is no one strange here except yourself, Peter Rugg," it said. "Time has placed us here. And the storm which you cursed and defied is spent at last. But your house, your wife, your neighbors are gone too. You were cut off from the last generation and you can never fit into the present. Your home is gone now and you can never have another home in this world."

When we looked at the carriage again, we saw it standing in the street; but the shafts rested empty on the road. And inside, upon the seat, there was a thick layer of dust and no sign of Peter Rugg or of Jenny. It was an old chaise, for 50 years idle and abandoned.

In Defense of His Right

Daniel Defoe

Daniel Defoe, English novelist (1661[?]–1731) One of the great early journalists of England was Daniel Defoe. He made it his business either to know or to invent the "inside story," so that anything he wrote about was made to seem very close to the reader. In his famous Robinson Crusoe, *you may remember, he knew exactly how Mr. Crusoe managed everything. He could create an amazing impression of reality in his narrative and make the most commonplace event interesting. Thieves, and rogues of many kinds, come alive in his novels.*

There was once a wealthy gentleman who had one son named Alexander. His wife died and he married again. His new wife had several children of her own, and these she favored greatly over the other child.

When the gentleman's own son, Alexander, asked her for permission to travel and see the world, she refused him flatly, because of the expense. But she was delighted when, after some discussion, he left on his travels without her permission.

At first Alexander's father heard from him regularly and sent him a regular allowance. But one day a bill was presented and the stepmother got her husband to refuse to pay it. The bill was sent back, unpaid.

From that time on, no more letters came from the son

and heir. The woman released the full powers of a scolding tongue to persuade her husband that Alexander ought to be disinherited—for neglecting his parents if he were alive. If he were dead,—well then, he couldn't inherit anyhow, and her own son should be the next heir.

She herself, and her own children, kept provoking the father until there was no peace at all in the family. At the least doubt, at the slightest word of indecision from him, their clamor increased, till he was nearly tortured into disinheriting his own son in favor of hers.

At last the man decided to fix a period of four years within which his son might make himself known again and save his fortune. She fought this with a perfect fury of abuse.

"You will never do justice to your other children. Your first child is the only one you care about!" she cried. "I hope his ghost comes to you some day and tells you with his own tongue that he is dead. May his ghost himself tell you he will never claim his estate."

"Even if my son is alive," answered her husband, "may his ghost appear to you before this year is out and make his claim. If injured souls can walk after death, why not during life as well?"

His reply only increased her anger further. And so loudly did she insist that he disinherit his own son in favor of hers within a single year, and not four as he had planned, that at last he had to consent.

The houses at this time were equipped with iron casement windows, opening outward, but shut and fastened on the inside. One evening, while the pair were quarreling violently about the lad's inheritance, a hand appeared at the casement and tried to force it open. The wife was thoroughly frightened.

"There are thieves in the garden," she yelled, and the good man ran to the door and peered out. "There's no one there," he reported. "I can see every part of the garden, and there's no one quick enough to have scrambled over the wall before I got there."

"I'm not drunk or dreaming!" the woman cried. "I know a man when I see one. He put a hand to the casement, and when he saw us in the room and he couldn't open the casement, he walked off."

The man was annoyed at this. "You're jumping at shadows. Maybe it was the devil. Or my son, come to tell you what a devil you are, to make me disinherit my own heir."

"If it was the devil, it was your son's ghost, come to tell you he was gone to the devil himself!" said the woman.

"Alexander!" the man called out. "Alexander, if you are alive, show yourself, and don't let me be insulted every day with your being dead!" At the very last word the hand returned to the casement. The window was flung open, and there was the young man looking full into the room with an angry face at his stepmother. "Here!" cried the face, and disappeared in an instant.

The woman shrieked dreadfully and fainted. Her husband ran again to the garden and again found no trace of anyone and every gate shut and bolted beyond question. A workman or two outside testified that absolutely no one had been near.

"What was it?" asked the woman when she came out of her faint.

"It was Alexander, to be sure," said the man, sitting there quietly and regarding her steadily. With that, she fell into a fit, shrieking and screaming horribly, and was ill for several days. Time hardened her mind, however, and sharpened her tongue. It was not long before the poor man could silence her only by threatening to recall the apparition.

At once she accused him of dealing with the devil and threatened to expose him as a wizard. That was no slight threat in the eighteenth century.

Next day he awoke with her words all forgotten, but she was still angry and full of resentment. She could not live with a man, she said, who could bring the devil into the room to murder his wife.

Sure enough, he soon found she had sworn a warrant against him, charging she was in danger of her life. Some of her friends were prepared to take him to the judge in spite of all he could say to soothe her.

The more frightened he showed himself, the more insolent she became over his witchcraft and sorcery. Friends were called in as judges to try and settle things, but they were useless.

His supporters insisted that the charges were simply made up. She insisted that he had threatened her with his son's ghost, and now had even made it appear. He had made the devil appear as his son. But if he should settle the estate on her son, she would withdraw the charge.

At that, there were further high words. But the upshot was that the gentleman signed a paper, saying that in four months' time he would rewrite his will or give himself up to the police for witchcraft.

Even in the presence of these private judges, he said, "Although I am signing this paper, I am doing so against justice, my conscience, and my reason. And I shall never do what the paper says, because I am satisfied in my mind that my son still lives."

"Let him sign," said the wife, "and then let me alone to make him perform the conditions."

"In my whole life, I have never dealt with any devil except one. She is sitting over there!" the man said, pointing his pen at the wife and signing the paper. "But neither she nor any other shall get it executed. Remember I say so!" Only the judges present prevented a renewal of their warfare.

At the end of the four months a day was appointed and friends were asked to witness the signing of the papers. New and old writings and documents of all kinds were brought out, and the father expressed himself ready. If his son were alive, he said, he was undutiful in not appearing.

They had just read and discussed the new deeds. According to the story, it was the wife, not the husband, who took up the old papers and writings to tear off their seals and destroy them, when a rushing noise was heard in the room, as if the hall door had admitted someone, and then shut. It was so distinct that all were surprised. Nothing could be seen, but the woman turned pale and asked her husband if he had summoned more devils.

"Have you heard anything from your son?" asked one of the friends. "Not a word these five years," answered the gentleman. "I know nothing of him, and could not write to him, because I have no address to which I may send a letter."

"I am convinced," said the friend, "that the son could know nothing of this meeting. But I am even more certain that there is some unseen thing in this room. I heard it distinctly."

"Yes. I felt a wind as it passed me," put in a second.

"And you have not heard your son's voice for five years?"

"Several times," the man answered, "I dreamt I spoke

with him, charging him with neglect and blaming his undutiful conduct. But even in my dream I heard no answer. My own question always awakened me."

"And what do you yourself think of it?" asked this friend. "Do you think your son is dead?"

"No indeed," said the father. "In my own conscience I believe he's alive as much as I myself am alive. In this transaction I am going to do as wicked a thing of this sort as any man ever did!"

"Truly, I don't know what to say," the friend and witness answered. "I don't like driving a man to act against his own conscience."

But the woman had recovered her spirits by that time and she reminded them of the purpose of their meeting. "I am not frightened. Come and sign the deed. Even if there were 40 devils in this room, I would destroy the old deed." And she picked up a paper to tear off the seal.

The window casement had been fastened on the inside, as everyone had noticed beforehand. Now it flew open and a shadow stood in the garden, the head reaching the casement. The face looked into the room, staring sternly at the woman, and cried "Hold!" And immediately the casement was clapped to again and locked inside, and the figure vanished.

This second apparition put the woman again into fits. Despite her defiance of 40 devils, this one spirit made the writing fall out of her hands. The two witnesses were also terrified but kept their heads. One took the fresh deed the father had just signed that turned the estate away from the son Alexander.

"I dare say the spirit will not be against our canceling this," he said drily. And he tore his name, written as witness, out of the paper. The other followed his example; and both arose, to announce that they would have no more to do with the matter.

But strange to say, the father himself saw nothing of this part of the proceedings. He was himself so frightened by the apparition that he fainted dead away—a fact which I particularly call to your attention, since it tends to disprove the charge of his wife, that he was linked with the devil.

About four or perhaps five months after these events, Alexander arrived at last. He had been in the East Indies, where he had gone four years before in a Portugese ship from Lisbon. At that time, there were no mail connections between England and the East Indies.

The young man was asked whether anything that had been done in this affair about his estate and inheritance had been known to him during his absence, or whether he had known of any apparitions or voices. He replied very positively that he had known nothing of the whole matter, and he had not had any experience which might have told him about it.

He had once dreamt that his father had written him an angry letter, threatening that if he did not come home he would disinherit him and leave him not one shilling. But, Alexander added, he had never in his life received such a letter from his father, nor for that matter, from anyone else.

The Three Rings

Giovanni Boccaccio

*Giovanni Boccaccio, Italian writer (1313–1375) Boc-
caccio was a poet and scholar in Italy. He had a flair
for finding or inventing tales that were full of life and
motion. Even though he turned them out by the hun-
dreds, there are no dull portions to be expected. He
collected so many stories from Greek, Latin, Oriental,
and European literature, that his* Decameron *is often
spoken of as a "source." This means that his tales made
other writers want to try their hands at the same things.
Among these other writers are Shakespeare and Chaucer.*

Saladin, Sultan of Babylon during the Crusades of the
twelfth century, was a great and brave man. He had reached
his high place through his own efforts, rising from a low
position in the state to be the sultan. Saladin was not a
particularly trustworthy person, nor soft in his dealings with
others; but he had a kind of rough justice.

The wars of this monarch were numerous and extensive.
They are still remembered in history, and like all wars, were
exceedingly costly. Year after year the treasury became emp-
tier and the condition of public affairs more alarming. At last,
Saladin himself felt obliged to look about him, and find a
way—no, not to cut down expenditures; that was unthinkable

in a king. Saladin began to look for a way of raising more money.

The state was poor at the moment, but the citizens were wealthy enough. And one citizen in particular came into mind whenever large sums of money were mentioned. He was Melchizedek, a Jew of Alexandria. At that time banking was not held in such high respect as a profession, so we shall have to call him a moneylender. Nevertheless, he was a wise man as well as an exceedingly rich one.

The sultan thought pleasantly of Melchizedek's wealth. But there was one great obstacle. What if this man should refuse to lend his money to the state?

Saladin's past plans had not been good business ventures. There was no real security to offer. Still, such a great monarch could not take away an honest citizen's money without some show of reason—after all, this was only the twelfth century. There had to be some way of forcing the gift. So the sultan reflected quietly upon all the ways in which a citizen might lose his property to his sultan, and soon he was contented.

That very day, Melchizedek received a royal summons to appear at the palace for a private interview.

"Honest man," said the Sultan to his visitor after they had spoken the preliminaries, "I have heard many reports concerning you. From many people I have heard that you are wise and particularly knowing in all matters concerning the highest kind of truth—I mean, in matters of religion. It is not often that the Sultan may speak with a man who is a great authority upon religion."

Melchizedek stood in dignified silence, as though he were overwhelmed by so much graciousness from his sultan.

"But since I have such a rare opportunity," continued Saladin, "I must be careful to make the most if it. There is a profound question I must ask you, whose answer has been the source of much strife and even bloodshed. When you have settled this question, your service to mankind will indeed be glorious."

"The question I shall ask is this, then: Which of the three great religions is the true one—is it the Jewish, the Moslem, or the Christian?"

Melchizedek realized that Saladin would pick a quarrel with him if he were to praise any one of the three more highly than the rest. He needed a reply that would avoid the trap.

*   *   *

The question Your Highness has asked is a vital one, and as you have so wisely warned me, too grave to be answered easily or lightly. I must beg you leave then to answer at length, with a fable which will make clear my thoughts upon this matter.

I have heard it told that once upon a time there lived a very great and wealthy man with several children who owned a supply of rare and precious jewels. One of the best of these, both in workmanship, and in the taste of its design, was a ring which he valued above all his other possessions.

Now it seemed to this man that the ring represented somehow the grandeur of his family, that it should never be separated from the estate, but should always go down with it from generation to generation. In order to accomplish this, he drew up a will which said that possession of that particular ring meant the inheritance of the whole estate.

Thus, the son who received this ring in his lifetime was thereby the proper heir and the head of the family. Lawful possession of the ring meant the whole inheritance. And he also wrote that whoever had the ring and the estate must will both in the same way to his heirs.

The family continued in great wealth and in public respect for generation after generation, and the will was respected by each heir. But it happened at last that the estate descended to a worthy man who had three sons.

And each of these sons was himself a worthy man; and no one deserved more than the others to receive the ring, and through it, the inheritance of the entire estate. All were equally dutiful to their father, and equally well-beloved.

Since the father loved all three of his sons he was unable to choose which son should inherit the ring. He promised it to each, in order to please them all. So he secretly summoned a fine jeweler to make two rings so like the first that none would know which was the original. And when he was dying, he took each son aside and gave him a ring.

When the old gentleman at last passed away, there was a scene of the greatest confusion. Each son produced a ring. There was no question in his own mind that this ring was the true one, so that the claims of his brothers astounded him. Each considered himself the legal heir but the case has never been settled.

Yet in just the same way, Your Highness, were the three laws given to his sons by God the Father, about which you have questioned me. How shall I give you your answer? Every one believes he is the true heir of God, having His law and obeying His commandments. Everyone finds truth and evidence to support his case. How shall I give you your answer? Which men are right is uncertain—just as the rings so skillfully distributed are still uncertain.

*   *   *

When Melchizedek stopped speaking, the Sultan Saladin sat deep in thought for a time, though his face did not reveal any displeasure. It seemed to him that this man had escaped the trap that had been set for him so truly and fairly that the sultan could not ignore it.

With the most gracious manner possible, the Sultan of Babylon told him of the trouble he was in: that his armies lacked supplies in a grave crisis and that money was needed immediately to save the state. He told his visitor, moreover, how at first he had thought of gaining his goods by forfeit through the use of his simple question.

Melchizedek gladly supplied the sultan with the money he needed. Later, Saladin paid him back in full, in addition to which, he gave Melchizedek wonderful gifts and maintained him in court in a grand fashion.

The Stone of Invisibility
Giovanni Boccaccio

There was once a simple-minded painter named Calandrino who lived in the city of Florence. He loved to hear strange stories, and he was never happier than when someone assured him very seriously that some wonderful tale which he had just been told was really a true one.

He had friends who kept company with him and amused themselves by tricking him. Bruno and Buffalmacco sometimes were merciless in kidding Calandrino, but the cruelest of their tricks was started by Maso del Saggio.

Maso and another fellow came up to Calandrino one day when the painter was busy looking at some paintings and statues. Maso winked at his friend and began talking about precious stones. From the way he talked, you would have thought that he had not even noticed Calandrino. Naturally, the painter wanted to hear what they were saying and he edged up closer.

"Truly a marvelous stone," Maso was saying. "Why, whoever can find it will be happy for life. He will—"

Calandrino could hardly contain himself. "Where are they? Where can I find them?" he blurted out.

The two "experts" looked surprised and a little doubtful. "In Nomansland, chiefly," Maso del Saggio replied finally. "In a region called Cornucopia. What a place! The grape vines are tied up with sausages. You can buy a whole goose for a penny. Why there—"

"Yes. Go on! Go on!" Calandrino urged him.

"—there you find a great mountain, and it is made entirely of grated Parmesan cheese. On the mountainside people do nothing but make macaroni and ravioli. They boil it in chicken broth afterwards. And then, of course, there's the river that flows by. There's not a drop of water in it."

"A river without water?" Calandrino's mouth hung open.

"Yes, of course," Maso went on. "It's all white wine.

"How far away is it? Have you ever been there? Are there any precious stones?" Poor Calandrino could hardly stop his questions to wait for the answers.

"Have I ever been there?" Maso replied. "Why, if I've been there once, I've been there at least a thousand times. Of course it's a great many miles from here. There are two different kinds of stones there. One, when turned into a millstone, is the source of all flour! But despite their value, I think as little of them as the people there think of emeralds, for they have a whole mountain of them. The second is a stone that professionals call heliotrope."

"The heliotrope?" Calandrino whispered the question.

"Yes. That's really a jewel! Anyone who carries it becomes invisible if he is out of sight when the stone is in his hand!"

"But—but—is that the only place one can get the heliotrope?" asked the painter.

Maso pretended to think a moment. "No," he said finally. "Sometimes—not very often, but sometimes, the stone can be found right on the plains outside this city, the plains of Mugnone. You can't tell whether it will be a big or a little stone; but you can tell when you find it, because it's always a black stone."

Calandrino seemed to lose interest in the talk, and began muttering to himself. "A black stone . . . black . . . any size . . . stone of invisibility . . ." Then he roused himself. "I beg your pardon," he said loudly, "But I've just remembered. Business. Some business I have to work on . . . nearly forgot it."

He dashed away, leaving Maso and his friend roaring with laughter.

Calandrino hunted up Bruno and Buffalmacco; he stuttered with excitement. "Follow me!" he cried. "We will be the richest men in Florence. There is a stone in Mugnone that makes people invisible! I heard it from an authority, and we can find it before anyone else does. Then we can put it into our pockets, and we can go into any bank in Florence. We can take all the money we please, and no one will see us. We'll be rich!"

Bruno and Buffalmacco wanted to laugh aloud, but they managed to keep straight faces. "What stone is it? What is it called?" they asked.

"What do we care about a name?" Calandrino cried. "Let's start off and find it! We can pick up every black stone we see, and then we don't have to know its name. Hurry! Hurry!

Bruno looked loftily at his excited friend. "But just think a moment, Calandrino," he said. "What time is it now? Noontime? And the hot sun of Florence is blazing right up over our heads. The fields will be dazzling, bright with sunlight. And everything we look at will seem white, nor black. Anyway, there must be many people there on weekdays. They might even guess our secret and find the stone first. Let's wait till the weekend and go early in the morning. Then colors will be clear to the eye. It will be a holiday to pick up stones, with no one around to trouble us."

Calandrino was impressed. "You are right! Ah, how good it is to have wise friends to correct my mistakes!"

And on Sunday morning, early, his friends followed Calandrino as he burst out of the city, through the gate of St. Gallo, and on to the plain of Mugnone. In a moment he had his pockets dragging with black stones; he had an apron through his belt, as a sack to hold more; by lunch time he was staggering around, loaded with the rocks.

Bruno turned to Buffalmacco as prearranged. "Where is Calandrino?" he asked. And, "Why, yes; where is he?" Buffalmacco chimed in. "I saw him here only just now."

"That rogue!" Bruno pretended to rage. "He must have left us for dinner, while we made fools of ourselves here, picking up black stones!"

"He's tricked us!" Buffalmacco agreed, gazing right past Calandrino. "We're the only fools who would believe a story like his!"

By this time Calandrino began jumping up and down with joy, as much as the heavy stones allowed him. He was sure that he had found his stone, that one of the black weights he carried made him invisible. He was all ready to go back to the city. Without saying anything to the others, he stalked off.

"Well, let's go back then," Bruno said, heaving a big sigh. "But that Calandrino—he'll never trick us again like this. If he were here right now I'd clip his heel with this pebble—so he'd never forget it!" And he took aim as he spoke. The pebble hit the painter right on the heel, and the poor fellow had to bite his tongue to keep from yelling with the pain.

"Yes," Buffalmacco agreed sadly. "I would too. I'd hit him in the back—like this—"

And all the way back to the gate of St. Gallo they pelted their friend with stones, pretending they were only talking about it. The gatekeeper was informed in advance about the joke. By the time Calandrino passed through, he was sure that he was invisible, because the gateman looked right past him, while the stones flew all around the poor fellow, hitting him again and again.

It was dinner time in Florence, so there was no one on the street to greet Calandrino. Bravely he carried his great stone collection right up to his own door and waited to watch his wife's surprise at not seeing him.

"The devil must have got you! Everyone's finished with

dinner!" she yelled, as soon as the door had opened. There was no question that *she* saw him.

Calandrino was so disappointed and angry that he blamed it all on the nearest person, his wife. He threw down all his stones. He pulled her hair, and he even began to beat her. His yells of anger mixed with her yells of fright aroused the whole neighborhood.

Bruno and Buffalmacco came up soon, but the painter was already upstairs. "Come on up!" he yelled, looking down from his window. They looked at the stones on the floor and at the poor frightened woman.

"What's the matter, Calandrino?" they asked innocently. "What are those stones for? Are you building a house? We thought you were a painter."

"If you were angry," Buffalmacco said, "you didn't have to leave us like fools on the plain, while you came home without a word to us."

This cheered the poor fellow up a bit. At least, for a while he'd been invisible! "You see," he began to explain, "first I found that precious stone, and then—"

His friends nearly burst with laughter as he described how he had started for home invisible, how the stones had really hit him, how the gateman had never even said a word to him. "I was invisible to everyone!" he said angrily. "No one saw me—not you, Bruno, nor you, Buffalmacco, nor even the gatekeeper—I was just getting used to it, and came home here, when this fiend of a woman, this wife of mine—women have the most accursed way of turning wonderful things back into nothing!—she saw me at once! Why, if not for her I could be the happiest man in all Florence and go everywhere without being seen. But she has made me miserable! I could—I could—"

The foolish painter was about to begin beating his poor wife again, but his friends held him back by force. "Let her alone! Let her alone, Calandrino," they said. "She has done no harm to you. You knew what women could do to magical spells, but you didn't warn her to keep away. Furthermore, when you found the stone, did you want to let any of your friends share it? No! You slunk away from the field of Mugnone, trying to hide even from us. And naturally, when you came to your own house, and wanted to hide from your wife and tease her—it was too much. The heliotrope lost its power. It's just a black stone now, like any other stone. And now, Calandrino, my friend—now we can all see you, just as you are."

With that explanation, poor Calandrino had to admit he was wrong. He stopped blaming his wife. But it was a long time before he forgot his grief at losing the Stone of Invisibility.

The Three Robbers

Lucius Apuleius

Lucius Apuleius, Roman commentator (about 125 A.D.)
In every age there are a few writers who can reveal the
silliness and brutality of their times so pleasantly and
entertainingly that they are praised for it. Such a man
was Lucius Apuleius, who laughed at and criticized the
Rome of the second century. He was born and raised in
Africa, where much of the Roman Empire extended.

It was a very fine feast, a sumptuous feast, but my slave
and I were a little too much affected by it. Our tongues
would not talk with their usual accuracy, and our steps would
not go just as we directed them. My friend Byrrhaena had explained the whole matter very well, though it was still a little
hazy in my mind. The next day, it seemed, was a religious
holiday of great importance in that city. It was a day sacred
to the god of laughter, and we had already begun to cele-
brate. That was it. Elaborate ceremonies were planned for
the morrow, she had told me.

"I hope you will think of something clever to amuse us
with tomorrow," she said quite earnestly. As well as I could
in my confused state, I promised to hit on something good to
honor their god.

But the hour was late then, and my slave had helped me to set out for home, after I had taken polite leave. What a zigzag way I had to travel to reach home! No, it was not even my own home, which made it harder. It was the house of my friend Milo, with whom I was staying for these celebration days. Darkness hemmed in our torches, and a great wind blew them. From around a corner a furious blast took us, and our flares were snuffed out. We had to stumble through the streets without a light.

When we came to the place at last, I stared through the darkness to make sure my eyes did not deceive me. Yes! There were three huge figures, making some sort of savage attack upon the entrance! Milo, my protector, and everyone in his house would be slain! Robbers were loose here!

I cried out to the three figures, who cared nothing for the noise, but only carried their assault upon the gateposts more fiercely. Stranger that I was in this city, there was nothing to do but draw my sword and attack them as fiercely as I could.

To my surprise, one after another of the robbers fell before my attack. In a little while their bodies lay before my blurred vision, riddled with great wounds. And I staggered into my room, breathing heavily, and flung myself on my bed. In a moment I had fallen deep asleep, my head filled in dreams with the cries of the three savage robbers.

Well, the next morning I woke up feeling miserable, the fumes of wine still pushing at my eyeballs, and the horrid sight of those three mutilated figures at the door, right there before me. Three native citizens killed by an outsider! What chance would I have before any judge in that district? They would say that I had simply committed a triple murder!

And soon enough my fears became real; there was a great rapping and pounding at my door.

"Get up in there! Come out of it, and unlock your door! We'll teach you a trick or two—butcher us on the public streets, will you?"

"Get him out of there!"

"Oh, he's there all right. We'll get him!"

No doubt of it. This was an angry crowd, with an ugly temper.

Police, judges, citizens rushed in without further ceremony, and two officers dragged me forth. The whole city seemed to trail at my heels, and shove me forward, until we reached the forum. My head was hanging down to the earth, it seemed—no, to the regions under the earth. Maybe, I thought, I shall be there myself very shortly.

We had gone clear around every city square, as victims do

before sacrifice. Only the dense mob at the forum prevented a quick trial. The judges were ready, but the whole mob cried out to them. "The public arena! Try him in the arena!"

In a wink the crowd pressed forward to the Coliseum. Aisles and galleries were swarming with people. Some dangled from the statues and columns, or perched dangerously upon ledges and cornices, utterly unconscious of risk. Police led me down to the pit, where the town crier shouted, "The public prosecutor! Let him present his charges!"

These were serious enough, I knew, but they seemed even more serious at this hearing. An old man of great dignity uttered them so forcefully that I asked in my heart whether I could clear myself! The old gentleman had been making his round of the city, it seems, and had actually witnessed the murders.

"Sword in hand," he cried, "this man attacked three defenseless citizens, and left them on the street writhing in pools of their own blood. It is your plain duty to convict this man of a strange city, for a crime which you would never forgive even to one of our own citizens!" And with this last telling blow, the public crier commanded me to speak if I could defend myself. It was hopeless, but somehow I managed to get out a few words.

"I know how hard you must view me, after my having killed so many of your neighbors. But hear me out of kindness," I begged. "I was returning from a dinner party last night—I had drunk pretty freely, I know—when right before the doors of your good neighbor, Milo, my own host, I saw a great number of thieves pulling the gates from their hinges. What could I do? They were bent on murder! I heard them myself. One cried out, 'Come on, fellows; no quarter! Kill 'em while they sleep! Dead men can't betray us! Cut 'em down if they resist! Stab 'em in their beds!'"

"What could I do? For my hosts as well as myself, I confess I was badly frightened. But I drew my sword against the savage villains, who stood against me. No—in fact they drew up in ranks before me—a whole blood-thirsty horde waiting to swoop down and destroy me.

"I opposed them single-handed. Their leader and standard-bearer rushed me and seized my hair with both hands, trying to bend me backward and beat out my brains with the paving stone. While he yelled for one of his friends to help, I skillfully ran him through with a lucky stroke of my sword. A second one clinging to my legs was finished by another stroke; and a third who still advanced, I stabbed. Then the others ran off.

"But I call you all to witness: it was in the interests of law and order I did this, and I saved one of your own citizens and his household from robbery and murder. Is that considered a crime? Why, those who say I killed three of your good citizens cannot even find any motive for my deed! Surely—"

Here I was so overcome by emotion that I could only stretch out my hands, to beseech them for mercy and justice. When I thought they must be moved deeply, I called out upon the Eye of Justice, the Light of Day, and the High Gods upon Olympus, raising my eyes at last to my judges, to see how they were affected.

Never was such barbarity shown to a poor unfortunate. The whole assembly began rocking with laughter at my poor attempts to defend my actions; nay, my very judges laughed till they wept. And Milo, my own host whom I had defended, was shaking with mirth—ungratefully mocking my misery.

Just then a woman in black rushed forward, wailing loudly. At the center of the arena she clutched a small child to her bosom. Then an older woman, dressed in rags, followed her, and they wept loudly together. They walked to the platform upon which were placed the bodies of my three victims, suitably covered; and they waved olive branches over them as they addressed the multitude.

"For the sake of humanity and justice—pity these unfortunate youths, cut down by a foreign savage! Do not deny to a lonely wife and to a mother this last comfort of vengeance! Help this unhappy child, left fatherless in his tender years! On the altar of law and order offer up the blood of this murderer!"

With this the chief judge arose to speak.

"Not even the prisoner dares to deny his crime, for which the full penalty must be paid. We shall still find out who were his accomplices. One man alone could never have overcome such fine, strong young men, despite his fantastic story. The slave who accompanied him has escaped. There is nothing to do but wring the truth from this criminal by torture. Only then will the whole city be safe from this dangerous and ruthless gang that threatens it."

As he returned to his bench, fire and the wheel were brought forth, and many iron instruments of torture. It was fated, not only that I perish, but that I perish piecemeal, most miserably. Meanwhile, the awful din of the women's lamentations filled my ears. One of them paused for a last utterance of hatred.

"Before you torture that prisoner," she cried, "let him look with his own eyes on the youth and beauty of his victims. When they are uncovered by their murderer, you will be filled with just anger, and give him the full penalty he deserves!"

Loud applause greeted her, and I was forced against my struggles and pleadings to advance to the platform and draw back the covering. One of the attendants bent my arm for me. Another held my head, so I could not help gazing upon my victims as the covering fell back. What a sight! What a change in my fortunes!

Up until then I was a slave in Hades, doomed beyond hope. Now I could only gasp in amazement and relief.

The bodies of my butchered victims indeed lay before me. But they had never been human bodies! They were nothing but three enormous bladders, three bags, still pierced in the places where I had aimed my courageous blows. My sword had indeed left fatal wounds, which I could now witness quite calmly.

But the general laughter, which had been held in bounds for the time, now burst forth like wind and fire. Some rolled in their seats, helpless with merriment. Others held their aching sides with their hands. By the time they got up to leave the arena they could laugh no more; their jaws were fixed into grins as they looked back at me in passing.

For my part, from the moment I had withdrawn the shroud, I stood frozen, as motionless as the columns. Milo, my host, roused me by a hearty clap on the shoulder. Then my tears of relief and anger flowed freely, and my voice was choked with sobs. He was decent enough, I confess, to lead me home by the more deserted streets, doing what he could to calm my nerves and soften my anger. Nothing he said could lessen my shame at having been made ridiculous.

Soon the judges themselves arrived in their full uniforms to make personal amends. They pleaded that after all, they had known my family for years, and understood fully their merit, and my own honesty. And since my name was so well known and respected, the treatment could in no sense be considered an insult.

But the festival of the day—the solemn celebration made each year to the god of laughter—depended upon novelty and surprise for its success. Their god of laughter, as they claimed, owed me a debt, and would always befriend me henceforth, while the city, for its part, would bestow unusual honor upon me.

My name was to be inscribed upon the list of the city's patrons, and in addition, my statue in bronze would be erected as a perpetual memorial to this successful celebration.

Reviewing Your Reading

A Germ Destroyer by Rudyard Kipling

Finding the Main Idea
1. The story is mostly about the way the viceroy
   (A) enjoys meeting Mellish of Bengal (B) enjoys a good laugh (C) finds a way to get rid of Wonder (D) spends his days

Remembering Detail
2. Mellish had spent 15 years
   (A) studying cholera (B) trying to annoy Wonder (C) trying to see the viceroy (D) destroying all the germs of cholera
3. Mellishe of Madras was
   (A) a single-minded crank (B) a viceroy (C) a doctor (D) an important government official

Drawing Conclusions
4. You can tell right from the beginning of this story that the viceroy
   (A) does not like Wonder (B) admires Wonder very much (C) is afraid of Wonder (D) would like to have Wonder's job

Using Your Reason
5. The viceroy told the story of Mellish and the powder so often because he thought
   (A) it was so funny (B) he could use it to get rid of Wonder (C) it might help Mellish (D) he was a good storyteller
6. Wonder decided to resign because he
   (A) was feeling ill (B) wanted to go back to England (C) knew the viceroy was making him look foolish (D) could not keep up with his work

Identifying the Mood
7. After his meeting with the viceroy, Mellish felt
(A) angry (B) upset (C) frightened (D) happy

Reading for Deeper Meaning
8. Which of the following terms best describes Mellish?
(A) Single-minded (B) Stupid (C) Amusing (D) Clever
9. Which of the following would the author agree with most?
(A) Opportunity knocks but once. (B) Luck is where you find it. (C) All that glitters is not gold. (D) Easy come, easy go.

Thinking It Over
1. Why was the viceroy so anxious to get rid of Wonder?
2. If you were Wonder, would you have resigned? Explain.
3. Which of the characters, Mellish, Wonder, or the viceroy, did you like best? Explain why.

A Bank Fraud   by Rudyard Kipling
Finding the Main Idea
1. The story is mostly about
(A) a narrow-minded Yorkshireman (B) banking in India (C) the climate in India (D) one man's kindness to another

Remembering Detail
2. Reggie Burke was
(A) an accountant (B) a bank director (C) a bank manager (D) a member of Parliament
3. Riley got his job in the bank because
(A) he knew Burke (B) he did such good work in England (C) his father had influence (D) he knew a great deal about India

4. Riley kept his job, even when he was too ill to do it, because
(A) the directors admired him (B) Burke did his work for him (C) he paid someone to do his work for him (D) his father's influence kept it for him

Drawing Conclusions

5. Instead of saying that there were "two Burkes," the author would have meant the same thing if he had said that
(A) Burke understood his job very well (B) Burke did not do his job very well (C) there was not enough work to keep one man busy all day (D) there was enough work for two bank managers

6. Burke forged letters from the directors to Riley because he
(A) was afraid of losing his job (B) wanted to keep Riley alive as long as possible (C) had nothing else to do (D) wanted to prove how clever he was

Identifying the Mood

7. How did Burke feel when Riley finally died?
(A) Sorry (B) Uninterested (C) Happy (D) Angry

Reading for Deeper Meaning

8. Which of the following describes Riley best?
(A) Kind (B) Generous (C) Narrow-minded (D) Friendly

9. The story suggests that when people are mean to you a good thing to do is to
(A) ignore them (B) be nice to them (C) lose your temper with them (D) make fun of them

Thinking It Over

1. Why do you think that Burke went to so much trouble over Silas Riley? Would you do the same for someone who had been so nasty to you? Explain.
2. Why was Burke such a good manager? Why was he so much better at the job than Riley could ever have been?

A Terrible Night by Anton Chekhov

Finding the Main Idea
1. The story is mostly about
   (A) how Christmas Eve is spent in Moscow (B) a spirit meeting (C) how Requiemov's imagination was stronger than his common sense (D) the undertaker's business problems

Remembering Detail
2. During the spirit meeting a voice spoke to Requiemov from
   (A) a saucer (B) a crystal ball (C) the ceiling (D) a chair
3. The undertaker hid coffins in the rooms of his friends
   (A) as a joke (B) because he did not have enough storage space of his own (C) to save himself from ruin (D) to frighten them

Drawing Conclusions
4. Requiemov was so frightened by the sight of the coffin in his room because
   (A) he was afraid he would have to pay for it (B) it was a young girl's coffin (C) it was such an expensive one (D) he was thinking about death

Identifying the Mood
5. As Requiemov walked through the streets of Moscow he was feeling
   (A) amused (B) terrified (C) angry (D) happy

Reading for Deeper Meaning

6. The story teaches us to
   (A) avoid business troubles   (B) believe in ghosts (C) laugh at our own fears (D) avoid helping our friends

Thinking It Over
1. Do you find this story amusing? Explain why or why not.

2. Requiemov claims that he does not believe in ghosts, but on the way home from the spirit meeting he feels very frightened. Why?

A Husk by Anton Chekhov

Finding the Main Idea
1. Which of these titles tells the most about the story?
   (A) "The Empty Shell" (B) "The Schoolmaster"
   (C) "Life in a Russian Town" (D) "Bielikov and Varinka"
2. The author is mostly interested in telling us about
   (A) schools in Russia (B) Varinka (C) a hunting trip
   (D) Bielikov's fear of life

Remembering Detail
3. Bielikov liked rules and limits because
   (A) he did not want people to be happy (B) they made life definite (C) it gave him pleasure to ignore them (D) he thought they would help him in his career
4. Bielikov visited the other teachers in their rooms because
   (A) he liked their company (B) he wanted to learn from them (C) it was a rule (D) they asked him to
5. Bielikov seemed to lose all interest in living after
   (A) Varinka laughed at him (B) he was dismissed from the school (C) he and Varinka were married (D) he was injured in his fall down the stairs

Using Your Reason
6. Bielikov was afraid of marriage because
   (A) he thought he could not afford it (B) it might get in the way of his teaching (C) it seemed unknown and dangerous (D) he did not like Varinka

Identifying the Mood
7. After Bielikov's funeral, most of the people who knew

him felt

(A) sad (B) relieved (C) frightened (D) happy

Reading for Deeper Meaning

8. Which of the following describes Bielikov best?
   (A) Adventurous (B) Tolerant (C) Limited (D) Inspiring

Thinking It Over

1. In what little ways did Bielikov show how afraid he was of life, and how much he needed to feel protected?
2. After Bielikov's death, the teachers found that they did not feel any freer. Why?

The Bet by Anton Chekhov

Finding the Main Idea

1. The author is most interested in telling us
   (A) about capital punishment (B) how the banker was almost ruined (C) how hard the prisoner studied (D) how the lawyer's views about life and freedom changed

Remembering Detail

2. The lawyer bet the banker that, for two million rubles, he would stay in solitary confinement for
   (A) 5 years (B) 15 years (C) 20 years (D) 10 years
3. At the end of the 15 years the banker decided to save himself from ruin by
   (A) murdering the lawyer (B) canceling the bet (C) leaving the country (D) giving the lawyer half the money

Drawing Conclusions

4. You can tell from the story that, at the beginning,
   (A) the banker valued money more than the lawyer did
   (B) the lawyer valued money more than the banker did
   (C) neither of them cared about money at all (D) they both had more money than they needed

Using Your Reason

5. The banker locked the lawyer's letter in his safe because (A) he did not want anyone to know why he really won the bet (B) it would become valuable (C) he did not know what else to do (D) the lawyer had asked him to

Reading for Deeper Meaning

6. At the end of the story, the lawyer was (A) happy (B) confident (C) disillusioned (D) proud

Thinking It Over

1. What did the lawyer gain during the years of his imprisonment? What did he lose?
2. What had the banker gained by the end of this story? What had he lost?
3. At the beginning of this story, would you rather have been the banker or the lawyer? At the end? Explain.

The Upper Berth by F. Marion Crawford

Finding the Main Idea

1. The story is mostly about (A) a drowning (B) the *Kamtschatka* (C) a ghost (D) the ship's doctor

Remembering Detail

2. When the ghost appeared, the cabin was filled with (A) shouts and groans (B) the smell of sea water (C) music (D) bright lights

3. The captain wanted to (A) keep the whole business secret (B) frighten Brisbane (C) pretend the whole story was a joke (D) blame everything on the ship's doctor

4. After seeing the ghost, the captain (A) threw himself overboard (B) said he would never sail that ship again (C) broke Brisbane's arm (D) went mad

Drawing Conclusions
5. Brisbane stayed in cabin 105 because he
   (A) did not want to share a cabin with the doctor (B) did not want to share a cabin with the captain (C) was too lazy to move his belongings (D) wanted to find out what was going on

Identifying the Mood
6. How did Brisbane feel when the porthole kept on opening?
   (A) Amused (B) Afraid (C) Angry (D) Excited

Reading for Deeper Meaning
7. Which of the following describes Brisbane best?
   (A) Brave (B) Cowardly (C) Excitable (D) Dull

Thinking It Over
1. You can tell almost from the beginning of this story that something strange is going to happen. How?
2. The author ends the story by having the cabin boarded up. Do you think that is a good ending? Explain your answer.

The Umbrella by Guy de Maupassant

Finding the Main Idea
1. The author is most interested in telling us about
   (A) the umbrella (B) the Parisian War Office (C) the characters of M. and Mme. Oreille (D) the insurance company

Remembering Detail
2. M. Oreille had a cheap umbrella because
   (A) his wife was too mean to get him a better one
   (B) they could not afford a better one (C) the other workers needed something to laugh at (D) he liked it
3. Mme. Oreille finally decided to get the umbrella repaired

when a friend told her that
(A) M. Oreille deserved it (B) the rain might ruin M. Oreille's clothes (C) she was being mean (D) the insurance company might pay for the repairs

Drawing Conclusions

4. You can tell from the story that the director agreed to pay for the repairs because
(A) he thought it was fair (B) it was the only way to get rid of Mme. Oreille (C) he felt sorry for Mme. Oreille (D) he felt sorry for M. Oreille

Using Your Reason

5. Mme. Oreille ordered the umbrella to be covered with really good silk because
(A) she was ashamed of the way her husband had been looking (B) she saw some that she really liked (C) someone else was paying the bill (D) she decided that they really could afford it after all

Identifying the Mood

6. How did Mme. Oreille feel when she walked into the insurance office?
(A) Confident (B) Proud (C) Excited (D) Afraid
7. How did the director feel when Mme. Oreille made her claim?
(A) Amused (B) Astonished (C) Bored (D) Pleased

Reading for Deeper Meaning

8. Which of the following would the author probably agree with most?
(A) Persistence pays. (B) No news is good news. (C) A rolling stone gathers no moss. (D) All work and no play makes people dull.

Thinking It Over

1. Mme. Oreille hated to spend money, yet at the end of

the story she orders the very best silk for her husband's umbrella, saying, "I am not particular about the price." Does this fit in with her character? Explain.

2. M. Oreille's friend told them that the insurance company would pay for any damage done by fire if it was done in the house. M. Oreille refused to take his umbrella to the insurance office to make a claim, but his wife went ahead and did it. Explain why you think M. and Mme. Oreille acted as they did.

The Stolen White Elephant by Mark Twain

Finding the Main Idea
1. The author is mostly interested in
   (A) telling us about elephants (B) laughing at the police
   (C) explaining how the police work (D) describing the British official

Remembering Detail
2. The white elephant was a gift from the King of Siam to
   (A) Barnum's Circus (B) the American president (C) the English queen (D) Inspector Blunt
3. Inspector Blunt described the case of the stolen elephant as a
   (A) joke (B) windfall (C) nuisance (D) challenge
4. The elephant was finally found
   (A) at the circus (B) at a funeral (C) in a haystack
   (D) hiding among the detectives
5. At the end of the story, the British official was
   (A) a rich man (B) angry with Blunt (C) a ruined man
   (D) a happy man

Drawing Conclusions
6. At one point the elephant was described as being "plastered with circus posters." This shows that
   (A) the elephant was not hard to find (B) the elephant

was tame (C) Mr. Barnum had agreed to pay the $7,000
(D) the thieves were from the circus

Identifying the Mood
7. When the elephant was stolen, the British official was
(A) pleased (B) glad (C) surprised (D) dismayed

Reading for Deeper Meaning
8. Which of the following describes the British official best?
(A) A clever banker (B) A simple-minded fool (C) An
adventurous animal trainer (D) A deep thinker

Thinking It Over
1. Which parts of the story poke fun at the police?
2. Does the author make fun of anyone or anything else
besides the police? Explain.
3. Do you like the author's sense of humor? Explain why
or why not.

The Celebrated Jumping Frog
of Calaveras County by Mark Twain

Finding the Main Idea
1. The story is mostly about
(A) Jim Smiley's animals (B) how Jim Smiley was
tricked (C) Jim Smiley's winnings (D) a mining camp

Remembering Detail
2. If Jim Smiley could not get someone to bet on the other
side of something, he would
(A) switch sides (B) give up (C) lose his temper
(D) keep on trying
3. Andrew Jackson won his fights by
(A) barking (B) grabbing the other dog's hind leg and
holding on (C) biting (D) chasing the other dog into a
pond

Drawing Conclusions
4. Jim won money on his frog mostly from strangers rather than people he knew because
(A) the people in the camp knew what his frog could do (B) the people he knew did not like him (C) strangers always had more money (D) Jim did not like to win money from people he knew

Using Your Reason
5. Jim started off by being "sort of idle and careless" when he was telling the stranger about the frog because
(A) that was the way he usually was (B) he did not want to bet with the stranger (C) he wanted to get the stranger interested (D) he did not like the stranger

Reading for Deeper Meaning
6. Which of the following describes the stranger best?
(A) Cunning (B) Stupid (C) Pompous (D) Self-righteous
7. Which of the following describes Jim Smiley best?
(A) Stupid (B) Mean (C) Persistent (D) Greedy

Thinking It Over
1. Why do you think that Jim Smiley won so many of his bets?
2. Is Jim Smiley a man you could admire? Explain.
3. Do you think that the person telling the story admires Jim Smiley at all? Explain.

The Empty Drum   by Leo Tolstoy

Finding the Main Idea
1. The story is mostly about the way Emilyan and his wife
(A) obtain great wealth (B) solve difficult problems (C) enjoy themselves (D) fool the king
2. Which title tells most about the story?
(A) "The Wicked Soldiers" (B) "The King's Cathedral" (C) "The Magic Wife" (D) "The Obedient Prince"

Remembering Detail

3. The king tries to get rid of Emilyan by
   (A) hiring a murderer (B) giving him impossible work
   (C) offering him half the kingdom (D) putting him in
   the army

4. Emilyan's wife tells him not to run away from the king
   because
   (A) it would be disloyal (B) she could not go with him
   (C) soldiers would find him (D) her mother was against
   it

Drawing Conclusions

5. At the beginning of the story, you can guess that
   Emilyan's wife was disguised as a
   (A) queen (B) milkmaid (C) frog (D) tree

6. You can tell that Emilyan gains the good will of his wife
   mainly by his
   (A) strength (B) kindness (C) good looks (D) quick wit

Using Your Reason

7. Instead of saying "neither look back nor ahead"
   Emilyan's wife would have meant the same if she had
   said
   (A) work hard (B) take your time (C) think only of
   the task at hand (D) pretend you are as strong as an ox

Identifying the Mood

8. How did Emilyan feel when the king told him to build a
   cathedral?
   (A) Angry (B) Sad (C) Scared (D) Confident

Reading for Deeper Meaning

9. Which of the following best describes Emilyan's relationship with his wife?
   (A) Trust (B) Pride (C) Excitement (D) Gaiety

10. Which of the following virtues is most rewarded in this
    story?
    (A) Bravery (B) Steadfastness (C) Justice (D) Reverence

Thinking It Over

1. Does it seem logical to you that a powerful king would go to so much trouble to marry a peasant woman? Explain. Are there any other parts of the story that seem to be lacking in logic? What are they?

2. At the beginning of the story, which character would you rather be? Why? At the end of the story which character would you rather be? Why?

The System of Dr. Tarr
and Prof. Fether by Edgar Allan Poe

Finding the Main Idea

1. The author is most interested in
   (A) describing the south of France (B) describing the character of M. Maillard (C) showing us how lunatic asylums are run (D) making fun of a lunatic asylum and the storyteller

Remembering Detail

2. Under Maillard's "soothing system," the patients were (A) always locked up (B) allowed to do exactly as they liked (C) ignored or badly beaten (D) set to guard one another's actions

3. The storyteller finally worked out what had happened in the asylum after
   (A) talking to Dr. Tarr and Prof. Fether (B) reading about it in a book (C) being locked up for a month (D) talking to the keepers

Drawing Conclusions

4. The author described the young lady's eyes as unnaturally bright
   (A) so that we will understand that she is in love (B) as a hint that all is not well (C) to show that she is espe-

cially attractive (D) as a way of emphasizing that she is in mourning
5. Maillard said that his new method owed much to the work of Tarr and Fether because
   (A) that was the truth (B) the storyteller knew them well (C) he had the keepers tarred and feathered (D) he was being very modest

Identifying the Mood
6. During the dinner party, the storyteller began to feel more and more
   (A) amused (B) angry (C) uneasy (D) happy
7. When they heard the noises in the main hall, the dinner guests were
   (A) surprised (B) terrified (C) annoyed (D) unaffected

Reading for Deeper Meaning
8. When Maillard said that the inmates never let in any visitors except "one very stupid young man" he was talking about
   (A) himself (B) the storyteller's friend (C) Dr. Tarr (D) the storyteller

Thinking It Over
1. How are the patients able to gain control of the asylum?
2. The asylum was not actually a very amusing place. How did the author make it seem rather funny and harmless?

The Sphinx by Edgar Allan Poe

Finding the Main Idea
1. Which title tells the most about the story?
   (A) "A Lack of Proportion" (B) "A Giant Insect"
   (C) "Plague in New York" (D) "My Cousin's House"

Remembering Detail
2. For a short time, both the storyteller and his cousin

thought that the monster's appearance was a sign that
(A) the storyteller was mad (B) something terrible was going to happen (C) the storyteller had cholera (D) the world was being overrun by monsters
3. After the storyteller had described the monster to his cousin, the cousin realized that
(A) the storyteller had bad eyesight (B) the storyteller was very sick (C) such a creature could not exist (D) it was only a small insect

Drawing Conclusions
4. The storyteller thought that the monster was huge because
(A) he had compared it to some trees it had passed (B) it was standing next to a battleship (C) he measured it (D) his cousin measured it

Using Your Reason
5. When the storyteller's cousin realized that the monster was only an insect, he started talking about distance because
(A) this was at the bottom of the problem (B) he did not want to frighten the storyteller (C) he did not really understand the problem (D) he did not want the story-teller to know the truth

Identifying the Mood
6. When he first saw the monster, the storyteller was
(A) puzzled (B) amused (C) horrified (D) pleased

7. When the cousin explained about the monster, the story-teller must have felt
(A) amused (B) annoyed (C) relieved (D) proud

Reading for Deeper Meaning
8. The story seems to be teaching us to
(A) be good citizens (B) be afraid of insects (C) be good to each other (D) look at our fears very carefully

Thinking It Over

1. Which of the two characters do you like better, the storyteller or his cousin? Why?
2. In this story, the author is talking about the dangers that come from the lack of a sense of proportion. Explain what he is saying in your own words, giving examples of what you think he is talking about.

Three Sundays in a Week
by Edgar Allan Poe

Finding the Main Idea

1. Which title tells the most about the story?
(A) "Getting the Better of Uncle Rumgudgeon" (B) "A Romance" (C) "The Clever Sailors" (D) "A Trip Around the World"

Remembering Detail

2. Uncle Rumgudgeon told Bobby he could marry Kate when "three Sundays come together in a week" because (A) he knew that Kate did not want to marry Bobby (B) he hated Bobby (C) Bobby was pressing him to set an exact date (D) Kate asked him to
3. The friends who helped Bobby and Kate were (A) sailors (B) lecturers (C) scientists (D) doctors
4. They got on to the subject of "three Sundays" by talking about
(A) poetry (B) stars (C) science (D) cards

Drawing Conclusions

5. Bobby tried to win his uncle's consent to the marriage with
(A) lies (B) arguments (C) flattery (D) trickery

Identifying the Mood

6. When Uncle Rumgudgeon made his statement about "three Sundays" Bobby was
(A) pleased (B) excited (C) appalled (D) glad

Reading for Deeper Meaning

7. All of the following describe Uncle Rumgudgeon EXCEPT

(A) positive (B) generous (C) cranky (D) ill-willed

8. The relationship between Bobby and his uncle was really one of

(A) hatred (B) suspicion (C) affection (D) pride

Thinking It Over

1. At the beginning of the story, Bobby lists what he thinks are his uncle's "few weak points." Do you think the story supports what he says? Explain.

2. Which character appeals to you more, Bobby or his uncle? Explain.

Con Cregan's Legacy by Charles Lever

Finding the Main Idea

1. This story is mostly about

(A) how the McCabe brothers fought (B) Harry McCabe's death (C) farming in Ireland (D) how Cregan got his land

Remembering Detail

2. Peter McCabe told Con Cregan that if Con would pretend to be his father Peter would give him

(A) a jug of whiskey (B) Con's Acre (C) five guineas in gold (D) half the property

3. When Peter made the guests leave at the end, he said it was because

(A) his father needed to sleep (B) the room was too crowded (C) so his father could die in peace (D) it was very late

Drawing Conclusions

4. You can tell that, when Peter McCabe came to visit Con Cregan, he was

(A) grieving over his father's death (B) trying to cheat his brother (C) trying to get Con to lend him some money (D) asking Con to buy the farm

Using Your Reason

5. Con Cregan's reason for asking if everyone was listening as he described the last point in his "will" was that he (A) was afraid he was losing his voice (B) wanted to be sure that he had witnesses to the gift to Con Cregan (C) knew it would annoy Peter McCabe (D) wanted his son to hear

6. At the end, Con agreed with Peter that it was all a joke, but he really meant (A) Peter could have Con's Acre back (B) he was going to tell everyone the truth (C) the joke was on Peter (D) he knew that no one really believed that he was Harry McCabe

Reading for Deeper Meaning

7. Which of the following describes Con Cregan best? (A) Shrewd (B) Brave (C) Dull (D) Stupid

8. All of the following describe Peter McCabe EXCEPT (A) mean (B) ill-tempered (C) greedy (D) honest

Thinking It Over

1. Are any of the main characters in this story honest? Explain.

2. Describe the character of Con Cregan. Is he someone you could admire? Explain.

Peter Goldthwaite's Treasure
by Nathaniel Hawthorne

Finding the Main Idea

1. Which title tells the most about the story? (A) "Castles in the Air" (B) "Old Scratch's Treasure" (C) "Peter Goldthwaite" (D) "Peter and his Partner"

2. The author is mostly interested in telling us (A) how Peter Goldthwaite found his treasure (B) about life in an American town (C) that you cannot live on dreams (D) about Peter's friends

Remembering Detail
3. Peter would not sell his property because he
   (A) wanted more than anyone would pay for it (B) was planning to build a mansion there (C) liked it too much (D) was planning to give it to Tabitha
4. The treasure turned out to be
   (A) useless paper money (B) silver (C) gold (D) valuable stamps

Drawing Conclusions
5. You can tell that John Brown kept an eye on Peter because he
   (A) was paid to (B) wanted part of the treasure (C) was a good friend (D) was curious

Using Your Reason
6. John Brown planned to have the court appoint a guardian to look after Peter's money because he
   (A) wanted to cheat Peter (B) hoped Peter would reward him (C) was asked to by Tabitha (D) knew Peter could not do it

Identifying the Mood
7. How did Peter feel when John Brown explained to him that his treasure was worthless?
   (A) Pleased (B) Suspicious (C) Unhappy (D) Glad

Reading for Deeper Meaning
8. All of these describe Peter EXCEPT
   (A) Optimistic (B) Practical (C) Foolish (D) Unworldly
9. Which of the following do you think the author would agree with most?
   (A) Practice makes perfect. (B) Out of sight, out of mind. (C) Distance lends enchantment. (D) Do not make dreams your master.

Thinking It Over
1. In what ways is Peter Goldthwaite an odd character? Explain.

2. Who was the better friend to Peter, John Brown or Tabitha? Explain.

Edward Randolph's Portrait
by Nathaniel Hawthorne

Finding the Main Idea
1. This story is mostly about
(A) Edward Randolph (B) Alice Vane (C) the Boston Massacre (D) a turning point in American history

Remembering Detail
2. The people of Boston were angry because
(A) King George was coming to visit them (B) they thought taxes were too high (C) they did not want British troops there (D) they did not like the lieutenant governor
3. Lieutenant Governor Hutchinson decided to
(A) allow the British troops to live in Boston (B) disobey the king (C) imprison the Selectmen (D) send a message to the king

Drawing Conclusions
4. You can tell from the story that
(A) some of the people of that time believed in witchcraft (B) no one living at that time believed in witchcraft (C) witchcraft was unknown at that time (D) Alice Vane was a witch

5. It seems that the lieutenant governor believed at least partly in the story of the curse because
(A) he left Boston the very next day (B) he wrote a letter saying so (C) his words on his deathbed suggested that he did (D) he told his doctor that he did

6. You can tell from the story that there is some connection between the signing of the king's order and
(A) Hutchinson's death (B) Edward Randolph (C) Mr. Tiffany (D) the Boston Massacre

Identifying the Mood
7. Of the following, who was not happy to see the face in the picture?
(A) Alice (B) Captain Lincoln (C) The Selectmen
(D) The lieutenant governor
8. When the lieutenant governor signed the king's order he felt
(A) afraid (B) glad (C) pleased (D) curious

Reading for Deeper Meaning
9. Which of the following meant the most to the lieutenant governor?
(A) Courage (B) Loyalty (C) Power (D) Friendship

Thinking It Over
1. Why should the face of Governor Randolph be important in deciding whether to give Castle William up to the British troops?
2. This story tells us about a basic American feeling about life. What is that feeling? Is it still important today? Explain.

The Devil and Tom Walker
by Washington Irving

Finding the Main Idea
1. Which title tells the most about the story?
(A) "Captain Kidd's Treasure" (B) "A Bargain with the Devil" (C) "Old Scratch" (D) "Deacon Peabody's Grounds"

Remembering Detail
2. As his part of the deal with the devil, Tom expected to get
(A) a new house (B) part of Kidd's treasure (C) Deacon Peabody's land (D) a large farm
3. The black mark on Tom's forehead was

(A) a small bruise (B) coal dust (C) a birthmark (D) the devil's fingerprint

Drawing Conclusions

4. The devil came for Tom because
(A) this was the date they had set when they made the bargain (B) Tom asked him to (C) Tom lied when he said he made no money on the transaction (D) he was tired of waiting
5. The story suggests that Tom would have been able to escape from the devil if he had been able to reach his
(A) burglar alarm (B) important papers (C) safe (D) Bible

Reading for Deeper Meaning

6. All of the following describe Tom Walker EXCEPT
(A) wise (B) vain (C) greedy (D) stingy
7. Which of the following would the author agree with most?
(A) All work and no play makes people dull. (B) Early to bed and early to rise makes one healthy, wealthy, and wise. (C) Nothing ventured, nothing gained. (D) Honesty is the best policy.

Thinking It Over

1. In what ways does the devil show that he is a "shrewd businessman"?
2. What is the author saying when he describes the state of the trees in the swamp? What do the trees tell us about Tom's neighbors?

The Specter Bridegroom
by Washington Irving

Finding the Main Idea

1. Which title tells the most about the story?
(A) "A Ghost Story" (B) "Robbers in the Forest" (C) "All's Fair in Love and War" (D) "The Mysterious Horseman"

Remembering Detail

2. Herman would not go to visit the Landshorts because
(A) his family and the Landshorts had been enemies for generations (B) the journey through the forest was too dangerous (C) he had better things to do (D) he was due at the cathedral in Wurtzburg

3. While most of the guests were enjoying themselves, Herman and the bride
(A) spoke not a word (B) spoke sadly together (C) quarreled and cried (D) ignored each other

Drawing Conclusions

4. When Herman finally arrived at the castle, he was rushed in because
(A) dinner was already very late (B) they were eager to hear why he was late (C) they knew he was not the count (D) a gang of robbers was riding close behind him

5. You can tell from the story that Herman and the bride
(A) already knew each other (B) disliked each other at once (C) fell in love at first sight (D) would never get on well with each other

Using Your Reason

6. The poor relatives laughed at the baron's jokes because
(A) they needed to keep on good terms with him (B) they thought they were so funny (C) no one else was allowed to laugh (D) they were the only ones who understood them

7. Herman pretended to be a ghost
(A) for a joke (B) to impress the bride (C) to get out of the castle alive (D) so he could make fools of everyone

Reading for Deeper Meaning

8. Which of the following describes the count best?
(A) Proud (B) Timid (C) Romantic (D) Pompous

9. All of the following describe Herman EXCEPT
(A) loyal (B) stupid (C) quick-witted (D) brave

Thinking It Over
1. How does the author make it seem that Herman's appearance at the castle is really that of a ghost?
2. Why is it hard for Herman to explain why he is really at the castle?
3. What kind of man is the baron? Explain.

Peter Rugg, The Missing Man
by William Austin

Finding the Main Idea
1. Which title tells the most about the story?
(A) "The Endless Journey" (B) "The Abandoned Carriage" (C) "Looking for Boston" (D) "The Terrible Storm"

Remembering Detail
2. Peter Rugg was always looking for
(A) his daughter (B) Boston (C) his horse (D) the Merrimack River
3. The auction of Peter Rugg's property was interrupted by
(A) Peter and Jenny (B) a terrible fire (C) a flood (D) Mrs. Rugg

Drawing Conclusions
4. You can tell from the beginning of the story that something strange is going to happen because
(A) the horses seemed nervous and disturbed (B) the coach was crowded (C) the storyteller had to ride next to the coachman (D) the passengers were all upset

Using Your Reason
5. Peter Rugg had only English money to offer the ferryman because
(A) he was born in England (B) he had just come back from England (C) Jenny had spent all his American money (D) he lived when the English king ruled America

Identifying the Mood
6. Throughout the story, Peter Rugg felt
(A) happy (B) angry (C) bewildered (D) confident

Reading for Deeper Meaning
7. Which of the following would the author agree with most?
(A) Out of sight, out of mind. (B) Pride comes before a fall. (C) If you can't beat 'em, join 'em. (D) He who laughs last, laughs loudest.

Thinking It Over
1. Do you think Peter was punished too harshly for his sin? Explain.

In Defense of His Right by Daniel Defoe

Finding the Main Idea
1. The story is mostly about
(A) Alexander's relationship with his stepmother
(B) Alexander's undutiful conduct toward his father
(C) Alexander in the East Indies (D) how ghostly doings kept Alexander's inheritance safe

Remembering Detail
2. Alexander's stepmother wanted her husband to leave all his money and property to
(A) Alexander (B) her own children (C) her friends
(D) herself
3. After the ghost appeared, Alexander's stepmother said she would have her husband jailed for
(A) witchcraft (B) mistreating her (C) beating the children (D) stealing

Drawing Conclusions
4. Alexander's stepmother was glad when he left on his travels, even though she had said he could not go, because
(A) she was very fond of him (B) he would come back

with lots of interesting stories (C) there was always the chance that he would never come back (D) now she could be sure of getting stamps from foreign lands

5. You can tell from the story that, in the eighteenth century,
(A) witchcraft was a joke (B) it was very dangerous to be accused of witchcraft (C) no one believed in witchcraft (D) it was an honor to be called a witch

Using Your Reason

6. The witnesses tore their names out of the deed because
(A) they did not approve of it (B) they were afraid of Alexander's father (C) Alexander's father asked them to (D) the appearance of the ghost frightened them

7. The ghost appeared when it did
(A) as a joke (B) to save the life of Alexander's father (C) by coincidence (D) to save Alexander's inheritance

Reading for Deeper Meaning

8. Which of the following describes Alexander's father best?
(A) Weak (B) Strong (C) Steadfast (D) Loyal

9. Which of the following describes the relationship between Alexander's father and stepmother best?
(A) Loving (B) Trustful (C) Reverent (D) Uneasy

Thinking It Over

1. Alexander's father promised to disinherit his son in order to get peace in his home. Do you think he did the right thing? What would you have done in his place?

2. Describe the character of Alexander's stepmother. Do you think she was right to try and get her husband's wealth for her own children? What would you have done?

The Three Rings   by Giovanni Boccaccio

Finding the Main Idea

1. Which title tells the most about the story?

(A) "Saladin the Sultan" (B) "The Three Religions"
(C) "Saving the State" (D) "Escaping a Trap"

Remembering Detail

2. Saladin needed more money because his treasury had been emptied by
   (A) war (B) robbers (C) loans to friends (D) everyday expenses
3. The father of three sons solved his problem by
   (A) disinheriting two of his sons (B) throwing away the ring (C) having two exact copies of the ring made (D) giving the ring to his eldest son

Drawing Conclusions

4. Saladin knew he would have trouble borrowing money because
   (A) no one in Babylon had as much money as he needed (B) he had not always paid back loans in the past (C) borrowing money was not allowed by law (D) he did not know how to go about it

Using Your Reason

5. Melchizedek was afraid of Saladin's great show of courtesy because
   (A) someone had warned him of what was going to happen (B) he was a very timid man (C) he was afraid Saladin had discovered that he had been stealing money (D) it made him suspect that Saladin was up to no good
6. Saladin's question was such a clever trap because
   (A) Saladin could change his religion at any time (B) religion was not permitted at all in Babylon (C) choosing one religion as the best would make enemies of the other two (D) there was only one religion in Babylon

Reading for Deeper Meaning

7. Melchizedek's story really deals with
   (A) religious toleration (B) democracy (C) the writing of wills (D) a father's weakness

Thinking It Over

1. By what means did Saladin hope to get Melchizedek's money?

2. How did telling the story help Melchizedek avoid the trap the Sultan had set for him? What points did it make?

The Stone of Invisibility
by Giovanni Boccaccio

Finding the Main Idea
1. The story is mostly about
   (A) the wonderful country of Nomansland (B) the emerald mountain (C) how easy it was to fool Calandrino (D) Calandrino's relationship with his wife and children

Remembering Detail
2. More than anything else Calandrino loved
   (A) money (B) strange stories (C) Florence (D) large paintings
3. As a joke, Calandrino's friends
   (A) pretended they could not see him (B) found the stone for him (C) said they would buy the stone (D) took the stone away from him

Drawing Conclusions
4. Calandrino's friends got him interested in the stone by
   (A) showing it to him (B) pretending it was a secret (C) giving him a picture of it (D) showing him books about it

Using Your Reason
5. The real reason Calandrino's friends made him wait until the weekend to look for the stone was because
   (A) they would have more time to look (B) the sun would not be so hot (C) Sunday was a holy day (D) there would be fewer people around to spoil the joke

Reading for Deeper Meaning
6. The best word to describe Calandrino is
   (A) clever (B) bright (C) wise (D) simple

1. What do you think of the author's sense of humor? Does it seem to you that there is cruelty as well as humor in the joke played on Calandrino by his friends? Explain.
2. Do you find Calandrino a believable character? Why or why not?

The Three Robbers by Lucius Apuleius

Finding the Main Idea

1. Which title tells the most about the story?
   (A) "A Sacrifice to the God of Laughter" (B) "The Perils of Drink" (C) "A Trial in a Roman City" (D) "A Roman Holiday"
2. This story is mostly about how
   (A) trials were run in Rome (B) a whole city played a trick on the storyteller (C) holidays were spent in Rome (D) too much wine can cause trouble

Remembering Detail

3. The storyteller attacked the robbers
   (A) for the fun of it (B) so they would not attack him (C) because he was vicious (D) to protect his host
4. He was made to look at the bodies of those he had killed at the suggestion of
   (A) his host (B) the judges (C) a relative of a victim (D) the crowd

Drawing Conclusions

5. You can tell from the story that at such a trial no use was made of
   (A) eyewitnesses (B) torture (C) judges (D) lawyers

Using Your Reason

6. The crowd laughed so much when the storyteller gave the exact words of the robbers because
   (A) what the robbers had said was so funny (B) they

did not understand him properly (C) everyone knew the robbers were really dummies (D) they knew the robbers had said something quite different

Identifying the Mood
7. When the storyteller realized that the dead bodies were really only dummies he felt
(A) glad (B) amused (C) scared (D) relieved
8. As the crowd left the arena, the storyteller began to feel
(A) insulted (B) excited (C) surprised (D) amused

Reading for Deeper Meaning
9. Which of the following do you think the people of the town would agree with most?
(A) He who laughs last laughs loudest. (B) Laughter is the best medicine. (C) Fools rush in where angels fear to tread. (D) You can lead a horse to the water but you can't make it drink.

Thinking It Over
1. What does the story tell us about life in this city and about this particular holiday?
2. What finally made the storyteller believe that the joke was not meant as an insult?
3. Do you think the storyteller found it easy to forgive the people who played this elaborate joke upon him? Would you? Explain.